ꝏ 3/14/99

To

Boo Boo

Reading is fundamental

Snake hunting is a must

Love

Vivian Allison

Footprints of the Garden Snake

Vivian Allison

VIVISPHERE
PUBLISHING

PUBLISHED BY VIVISPHERE

 Published in the United States by Vivisphere Publishing Company
PO Box 98
Accord, NY 12404

http://www.vivisphere.com/

ISBN 1-892323-02-8

Library of Congress Catalogue Number 98-85376

Manufactured in the United States of America

The book is set in Adobe Apollo, a highly readable face designed by Adrian Frutiger in 1961 for the Monotype Corporation. Designed and typeset in the foothills of the Adirondacks by the folks at *Syllables*.

Cover design by Crescent Hill Graphics
Brooklyn, New York

A special thanks to those from whom I've learned much.
Andy Demsky, Peter Cooper

For

Chris, David, Joe, Doug, Stephanie, Elizabeth,
Summer, Candra, Lisa, Ashley, Justin, Christopher.

In The Beginning

Thrashing. Fighting his way through an exotic jungle of crackling, slashing greenery, branches, broad dark leaves, bowing thorn trees, slapping vines, dangling, prickly unripened fruit, a booming voice at his back. A voice that seemed to rocket through the underbrush and knock the wind out of his chest.

He ran ducking, dodging, falling, scrambling.

Small, sly lizards scattering at his naked feet. Swarms of gnats catching like crumbs in his eyes, his throat. A dense humidity pressing in on him. Breath coming in gasps. A rain-forest thickness binding his chest.

His hands swung at walls of vegetation, frantic, lunging deeper into the darkest part of the jungle.

Still the voice boomed and ranted at his back. A forceful beam of sound, a solid thing, like a giant avalanching boulder crushing and thundering down from behind.

He fell again, picked himself up and looked down at the blood seeping from his knees, smudged with green from fighting through giant ferns, scrambling over moss-covered rocks. Chattering, cheering monkeys thrashed in the treetops overhead, pelting him with half-chewed fruit and gray, seed-filled feces.

He looked around, frenzied, pulling matted leaves out of his eyes. He called out her name. Where was she?

Where had she gone? Where?

Slowly, slowly the dream grew smoky, intangible, curtains of nothingness rising up like steam from the hot jungle floor.

Concho rolled over, reached for his pillow. His hand hit something hard, burning hot, and he winced. His back ached from lying on something bumpy and rigid beneath him. Sweating and uncomfortable, he moved his foot to kick off the covers. His feet waggled in the air.

No pillow. No blanket.

Concho's eyes felt crusty, sealed shut. Gritty dust and thick saliva gunked up his teeth like old 40-weight motor oil. He blinked. Blinked again. Got one eye open.

A white-hot noontime sun breathed invisible fire out of the wide, featureless sky. The earth all around him was liquid with heat waves. A parched, burnt-grass, withered-tree landscape.

Where was he? This was no rain forest! Perhaps that had been the dream's purpose: to transport him for a short time out of this blast-furnace reality. The breathing here came just as hard. Shallow gasps. Each inhalation tanning the back of his throat like leather. He coughed and his throat made the sound of a paper bag crinkling. Dang. A hundred times dang. Wherever this place was, whether this was a dream or not, it was only a different kind of hell. From a hellish jungle to a hellish desert. Maybe if he closed his eyes and allowed himself to drift off again, he'd find himself in yet another part of the world. Perhaps a place more to his liking.

His eyes roved the scenery. So dry, surreal, no sign of life.

Wait! Hold on! Right at his feet, a creature stirred.

"Hello. Tho, you are alive."

Concho closed his eye again. Damn. It felt weird to be dreaming that he was trying to wake up. He clenched his fists, forcing himself to stay prone.

"You're not dreaming." The voice sounded like someone he had known a long time ago. A college professor.

Did he dare risk opening his eyes again? What if it was still there? What if it was still talking to him? That *thing*.

He wouldn't respond. That was it. He'd ignore it. He wouldn't say a word. Shoot. He could hear it moving closer, small mounds of sand making that gritty moving-aside sound.

"How do you know I'm not dreaming?" Concho said, eyes shut tight, muscles tense.

"Becauthe I'm not athleep."

Concho scrunched up his face. Tricky stuff this....College professor voice coming out of *that*. His pulse quickened. Okay. This was okay.

Concho cleared his throat and spat a sticky glob. "Okay," he said, trying to control his heart rate, "you may not be asleep, but if you were part of my dream, you'd believe you were awake, wouldn't you? I mean, you wouldn't know the difference, would you?"

The chuckles undulated slowly toward Concho, the small hairs on the back of his neck rose up.

"You're not athleep."

"Then I'm crazy."

"Open your eyeth."

"Nope. Don't want to."

"I won't hurt you."

Starting with slits, Concho gradually worked his eyes open all the way. Yep, still there. Now what?

Just as before, a huge rattlesnake. Only now it was coiled up a few feet from his face. Concho judged the creature to measure about seven feet in length. Its fat, scaly body glistened dully in the brilliant sunlight. The snake's head rose slowly higher, about two feet and it cast a thick, tapering shadow. He met the snake's even gaze, squinting.

"Thee. Not tho bad," the snake said, its split tongue pushing out the words.

"Maybe not for you, but imagine how I feel waking up in the middle of...wherever this is."

"Texath."

"Texas. Dang. See, now that's why this has to be a dream." Concho sat up halfway, wiped the sand from his forearms.

"Explain, pleathe."

"Well, it's bad enough waking up to a conversation with a snake. But I went to sleep in...uh...in...." He looked away as if searching for the name of the place somewhere in the sand.

The snake waited.

Concho tried to speak, his mouth half-way open, his tongue twitching, aching to say the name of the place he was from.

"In?" the snake queried.

"In...." Concho's face twisted to one side. "Damn! I know it has *sin* in it."

"Oh. Sodom? Gomorrah, perhapth?"

Concho shook his head. "No, it's—dang, I know it—it's something, something sin."

"Well," the snake began, "I really don't care."

"Wisconsin!" Concho blurted. A smile of triumph wrapped around his face. "Wis-con-sin! See! Something, something sin. See I told you. Wisconsin!"

"What'th a with-con-thin?"

Concho surveyed the strewn limestone rocks, scrubby bushes and arid wasteland around him. "A place far, far away, I would guess," he said, at last.

"Oh." The snake sounded, for a snake, bored.

Concho eyed the creature, sat up the rest of the way. His back arched as he stretched and rubbed his shoulders. He reached around and pulled several large burrs from his shirt. Images from his dream still played out in his mind—wide, waxy leaves, slender vines, shrieking monkeys. And that thudding, thunderous voice bawling after him. Was that Wisconsin? His mind rocketed images at him like a fiendish slide show, all fuzzy and out of focus, but full of razzle-dazzle color. Finally his brain signed off and went completely and serenely blank.

Hmm, that was better.

Odd.

Now this talking reptile. Better deal with it, get it over with.

"So, what are you, some kind of guardian snake, or something?" Concho asked.

"I am a rattler, not a garden thnake," the snake answered huffily.

"Guar-di-an. Guardian. You know, to watch over me while I slept."

Again that serpentine chuckle. "Not hardly."

"Then how is it you can talk?"

"Don't know. Maybe I'm not talking. Maybe you're understanding me and I'm not talking."

Again, Concho scrunched his face, then scratched his scalp. His hair was full of sand.

"In that case," Concho said, stretching himself, "maybe you're the one who's dreaming."

"No. I'm awake. I knew you were coming."

"How'd you know I was coming?"

"I knew a human would be coming, that'th all. Didn't know it would be you."

"You know how I got here?"

"Nope."

"But you do know why I'm here."

"I think tho."

"Care to *thhare* it?" He shook his head. "Share it with me?"

The snake's head made several loops—a Fokker escaping a Sopwith—the tongue spitting red lead. Concho looked away.

"Stop it, you're making me dizzy."

"Thorry."

"You didn't answer my question."

"Not an eathy quethtion to anthwer."

"Try."

"You like appleth?"

"What?"

"Do you like to eat appleth?"

"No. Not really."

"Why not?"

"Don't know, just don't. What's that got to...?"

"That'th why you're here."

A breeze shifted Concho's mat of reddish blond hair and he reached up and pushed a hand through it. "This don't add up. I go to sleep in Wisconsin, dream about weird stuff, and wake up in Texath, Texas, next to a talking snake...." His eyes clouded. "Because I don't like apples?"

"Thomething like that."

Concho rubbed his chin, glanced up at the sun, lay back down on the ground and closed his eyes.

"What are you doing?"

"Going back to sleep. This is the stupidest dream I ever had."

He heard the snake slither closer to him. Concho opened one eye, sat up with a jolt. The snake's jaws were open wide, exposing long, curved fangs and a wide, watery mouth the color of boiled chicken.

"What are you doing?"

"I'm going to bite you. It'th a favor, really."

"Hey!" he leaped aside, upright, on his haunches. "You could friggin' kill me!"

"Yeth."

"That's no kinda favor!" Concho grabbed up a jagged rock and instantly dropped it. "Ow. Dang, that's hot."

"Actually it ith a favor." The snake's head bobbed in the hot breeze. "If I let you live you'll go around telling everyone that you met a talking thnake. They'll think you're crazzzee. After a while, you'll begin to think you're crazzzee too. Then you'll wind up in one of thothe big placeth for humanth who are nutth. Thought I'd thpare you all that."

"I don't think I need your help, fang-face."

The snake's coils began to loosen and slowly, evenly the head began to lower. The tiny, gleaming snake eyes staying on Concho.

"You need my help. We need each other's help," the snake said in a low, throaty murmur, followed by a slow ticking sound. Like a stopwatch, or the tapping of Father Time's impatient fingers.

Without thinking, Concho's hand went to his stomach. All of a sudden he felt ill.

The snake nodded. "Take a look around. No roadth, no Coke machineth, no Burger Kingth...."

Concho's eyes rolled from one side to the other, search lights looking for escape routes.

The snake's unhurried, humming voice continued, "... rockth, cacti, Jack Rabbitth, thorn busheth, greathwood, dry boneth...but, of courth, I forget, you're Concho from With-con-thin...you don't need my help."

"How do you know my name is Concho?"

"You said it...earlier."

"No I didn't."

"Yeth. Yeth, I believe tho."

The coils loosened further, his rattles shook, and the snake's head bobbed toward the ground, a preparation for leaving Concho to fend for himself.

"Hey, uh," Concho sat back down, crossing his legs. "You got a name?"

The snake hesitated. "DeBack."

His eyes crinkled up. "Funny name."

"Not really, if you think about it."

Concho shrugged. "Okay, so, why don't you tell me why I'm here and how I'm suppose to help you."

The large, triangular reptile head rose up. "Thimple, really. Just two thingth. The firth ith to pick four pruny appleth off that tree behind you."

Concho shifted his body, his eyes moved up the trunk. The tree looked dead. No leaves, just four sick-looking fruit like over-sized figs hanging from the fingers of a black skeleton.

Concho looked back at the snake, then back at the tree. This was it? Climb the tree, pick a few apples that looked like God's dingle berries?

Concho gasped. "Well, shoot, why didn't you tell me it was somethin' simple like that? Hell. I can do that for you right now."

"Wait," DeBack hissed. "You can't pick the appleth unleththth you agree to help me with the thecond part."

"Okay, okay. Spill." Relief flooding his soul.

DeBack hovered, his unblinking eyes trained on Concho. "You have to tell me thomething firth."

"What?"

"Two thingth."

"What?"

"Maybe three."

"What? What? What?"

"You ever killed a thnake?"

Concho's eyebrows rose as he tried to think back over his life—to open up that part of his mind that held the past—and drew a blank. He blinked, concentrated, looked upward, rolled his eyes, moving deeper into that valley of memories, paging back through the years, taking a breath, squinting, furrowing his forehead, pooching his lips, snapping his fingers. Nothing. White space. Trying to picture anything that happened more than five minutes ago was like looking through a diary full of blank pages.

"No," he said after much thought. "I don't think I've ever killed a snake."

"Why not?"

"No reason. Same as eating apples, I guess." He shrugged. "What else?"

DeBack nodded. "Tell me, what do you want more than anything in the world?"

A blinding light hit Concho's brain. He winced and bent double, covering his eyes. His chest clamped shut and he struggled and gasped, trying to breathe. It felt like someone was stabbing him in the back of the head. After several moments, his breathing began to return in noisy bursts. He looked over at DeBack with bloodshot eyes, wincing.

Two red spots glimmered in DeBack's eyes.

"That ith not a quethtion that thhould hurt."

"I know." Concho rubbed both sides of his head. "Ouch." He swallowed, took deeper breaths and moved back to a sitting position, his legs extended, the worn soles of his boots pointing toward DeBack. Trying to act casual.

"Look, just tell me what the second thing is you need me to do, okay?"

DeBack nodded. "I want you to accompany me to a plathe called Wathhington, Dee.Thee. You know it?"

"Yeah, sure. Been there, I think. Or did I see it on something? A TV?" He paused and shook his head in frustration. His brain, empty and unyielding. "What am I supposed to do, carry you in a bag?"

DeBack's head moved back and forth. "Will you do it?"

"Well, it's either that or...." He indicated the barren landscape. "Turn into a Tater Tot out here."

He amazed himself. What in the world was a Tater Tot?

"No. I will not let you die. If you dethide to leave right now, you will thurvive."

"But you said..."

"There are thingth even I don't know about. Jutht decide."

Concho nodded, stood and stretched. He jumped several times trying to seize a lower limb of the stunted West Texas apple tree. No luck. He spit in both hands, locked his legs around the trunk and used his knees and feet to shinny up the tree. Brittle pieces of bark snapped off as he made his grunting, scraping ten-foot ascension.

"What are you doing?" DeBack asked, watching Concho's wiry climb.

"You said the first thing was to get these pruny apples."

"You don't have to come with me."

"I know," he grunted. Concho reached across and picked the first one, dropped it inside his tucked-in shirt. Then, stretching further out, he picked the other three and scrambled down to the ground.

"Okay," he said, panting. "Part one is done. Now what?"

"Put the appleth on the ground, then go over to that thtream and have a drink of water before you path out."

Stream? Concho turned toward a gentle gurgling sound. Had a stream been there all this time? He walked down the little gully, his boots crunching over limestone gravel and bent over the water. It looked pretty good, didn't smell brackish. Just a cool, rapid little stream running over a bed of smooth stones. No moss, no grungy, slimy, frog-egg stuff clinging to the edges.

He knelt and scooped some water into his mouth. It was cool and clean and he sucked down mouthful after mouthful, clearing away the dirt and grime and thick saliva. This was a Godsend. He filled both hands and splashed the back of his neck. Wetting his handkerchief, he cooled under his arms, wrung it out, tied it around his neck and walked back to the tree. But DeBack was gone and one apple was missing.

"Hey," he called out. "Where'd you go?"

"I'm right behind you."

Concho turned, shook his head and blinked several times.

"What the...? Wait a damn minute. This *is* a dream."

"No dream. Come on, we have to get to Washington, D.C."

DeBack went several yards, then turned to look at Concho.

"Aren't you coming?"

"'Course."

"What are you waiting for?"

"Nothing."

"And bring the apples."

"Sure."

DeBack turned and started off again. Concho hurried behind him, trying to keep from staring at the muscular, brown-skinned, naked man who called himself DeBack.

Walking behind DeBack was a dizzying affair. Concho found himself staring at the brown, gnarled feet as each unerring step missed a sharp stone, spiny cactus plants or other strewn and growing treachery. He watched DeBack for any signs of his true snake nature. He didn't know exactly what he was looking for—a swaying gait perhaps, a slithery quality—something that would betray him. To his amazement, and to a kind of low-wattage horror in the pit of his stomach, he picked up nothing. DeBack gave every appearance of being a fit, active nudist out for an afternoon hike.

Vague impressions bombarded his brain again—scenes where people turned into animals. Okay, okay. It's coming. In movies? Yes! What was the word for that? Shape shifting! Something that Indians were suppose to be able to do. William Hurt had turned into something fancy and furry in *Altered States*. And vampires turned into bats and Pinocchio had turned into a donkey. But in those cases it had gone human-turns-into-animal. Not animal-turns-into-human. And these had been stories exploring the animal side of being human, but this...this was something altogether new. And unholy, somehow. A law was being violated here. He could feel a kind of tension, as if the eyes of God were on them.

He shivered. With each step his mind seemed to remember how things worked. Technology. The car, electricity, the telephone....And how was it he knew about Tater Tots? Weird. Yet he couldn't remember how he got to this place.

Being alone with this naked, laws-of-the-universe breaker, this snake-man, in a desolate, unpeopled, moonscape place made Concho's toes knuckle-up inside his boots. He felt roped-in and squirmy. He glanced around from time to time, turning his head discretely, sharpening his senses, watching for some sign of civilization. A dirt road. A pickup truck. A group of school children on a geology field trip. Anything that would ease the gnawing suspicion in his mind about being drawn farther and farther from human habitation. Suddenly the idea of going to Washington, D.C. where normal people lived and police officers presided and places to hide abound seemed like an especially good one.

The wind picked up and off in the distance Concho could see a storm brewing, readying itself to blast across the West Texas landscape and wash the two of them away.

His eyes followed the line of clouds, towering like the Cliffs of Dover, his gaze moving farther off. There seemed to be a glimmer of a town or two, to the far left, but DeBack was heading in the opposite direction toward the hills.

"Excuse me, uh, DeBack," he called out, trying to keep up.

"Yes."

"If you want to get to Washington D.C., we should be heading toward a town."

"Agreed," he called over his shoulder.

DeBack skidded down a barren slope, unloosing a small avalanche of rocks and reddish dirt clods.

"Well, where're we going?"

"You don't expect me to go naked, do you?"

Good point. Concho hadn't expected a rattlesnake to walk anywhere, under any conditions, so he didn't have a ready reply and followed in silence. After another ten minutes of brisk travel across dry, hardened soil with withered underbrush they skirted a large triangular shaped knoll. DeBack pushed through the chaparral and pointed to a big hole in the side of a hill, just ahead of the storm that was stomping across the flatland toward them.

"We'll ride out the storm in here."

"What's this?"

"A cave."

"I can see that. Why here?"

"Patience."

♌♌♌

Concho followed DeBack a few steps inside, then he paused to look out. Whirling gusts carried debris into the air. The wind then calmed, but dust hung like an orange curtain overhead. The whole sky seemed readying itself to pounce. Concho shuddered. He didn't like the idea of going into an unlit cave with this snake person, but it seemed the better of his choices as he watched sparkles of lightning flash within the approaching embankment of darkening thunderheads.

He heard a chink, chink, chink.

"What're you doing?"

"Making light."

Through the last dim rays of the sun flickering inside the mouth of the cave Concho saw DeBack on his muscular bottom, striking two rocks together. Red sparks flew off in all directions.

Concho dug around in the pockets of his jeans. "Here."

"What's this?" DeBack asked, drawing his head back, squinting.

"Matches."

"Show me how they work."

Concho peeled one off and struck it against the flint. A soft yellow flame erupted from the twig of paper. DeBack pulled away, hissed softly then grinned.

"Yes, now I remember." He held up a small, blackly-singed torch. "Here, light this."

Concho held the match under the round head of the torch, smelling of tar and kerosene. When the torch caught, the yellow light illuminated a gypsum cave many times larger than he had anticipated. A high canopy of dull rock. The light seemed to catch in waves across the ground. Concho knelt and ran his fingers through the channels.

"What is this place?"

"My home."

Concho nodded. At last, something made sense. The home of a snake. Moist, dark, secret. He again traced the locomotion of the rattlesnake along the cavern floor. Deback's many journeys had caused the soft, white gypsum dust to bank in small, wavy mounds.

He glanced over at DeBack holding the torch.

"You're a snake, right?"

"Yes."

"And this is your home?"

DeBack nodded. "Right."

"So how come a snake's got a torch waitin' for him at home?"

"Foresight."

Concho nodded. Quick. Very quick. "Another thing, what happened to your lisp?"

"Lisp?"

"Yeah, say Washington, D.C."

"Washington, D.C."

"That's what I mean. When we first met, you said, Wathhington, Dee.Thee."

"When we first met, my tongue was split." He waggled a fully-formed, pink tongue. "It's hard for a snake not to lisp."

Concho nodded. This DeBack was sharp. A little too sharp perhaps. So, why did he need a human? A real human? The only sign DeBack had given of his true reptilian nature had been that little hiss of surprise when he'd struck the match. Otherwise anyone would be fooled by his homo-sapiens appearance.

And another thing. DeBack could have gotten those apples some other way. Can't snakes climb around in trees? Seemed weird. There was something funny about all this. Pieces were missing. Questions were piled chest high. Like, where had he come from? His memories were faint, shimmering scenes of people without faces.

He had remembered the name Wisconsin, with some effort. Nothing else about himself had pushed itself to the surface except *his* name, and that with DeBack's help. Was he married? Did he have kids? Did he have a job where people were standing around the water cooler, checking their watches and saying stuff like, "Where the heck is Concho?"

There was a word for this kind of mental block. He couldn't remember what it was. But it was a very specific medical condition.

Something very out-of-sorts here. Had he been drugged? Kidnapped?

He felt edgy, alert, watchful, but strangely unafraid. His nerves crackled with energy. Like a computer must feel plugged in for the first time.

Stay alive, that's what he had to do. Just stay alive.

Concho stared for a moment at the illuminated walls of the large cavern. Crudely carved, but clearly depicted petroglyph scenes of people and places covered the sides of the cave.

"Tell me what's on your mind," DeBack said, slipping into a pair of pants.

"What are these?" Concho gestured toward the walls with his hands.

DeBack chuckled. "Memories. Things that have been."

Concho's eyes swept along the glyphs, "Wish I had some memories about myself," he murmured.

As he moved toward the back of the cave, his eyes stopped suddenly at a scene depicting two figures under a scrawny tree that held four shriveled apples. One of the figures was a surprised-looking guy in boots talking to a large rattlesnake.

"What the?" Concho stammered. "Hey, *hey!* This is *us*. This just happened."

DeBack squinted in the dim light, focusing on the glyph.

"Ah, so it is." He resumed fumbling with the buttons on a shirt.

"But that *just* happened...." stabbing his finger at the glyph.

"Don't touch that," the snake man said. "You have no idea of its power."

"Well, seeing as how I ain't got no idea about nothin'...maybe you should start talkin'."

DeBack cleared his throat and launched into a detailed explanation of the relationship between present events and the past, how the two are connected and share an equal space in the continuum of time and how, indeed, the nature of time itself is like a logarithm that....

Concho lost the thread. His thoughts were racing. Perhaps there were more scenes, more incipient events, more stuff on the verge of becoming. Things of great importance. Things he, Concho, would be involved in. Things he needed to know.

He glanced over at DeBack, still preoccupied with his human clothing, saying something about loganberries.

Furtively, Concho headed deeper into the cave. Along the walls, he could see dim outlines of etchings. But even holding the torch close to the rock revealed only pieces of drawings, bits of line, scattered curves, as if his vision had closed to pinholes and he had to search the etchings in order to assimilate all the details. As he crept farther along, the darkness became deeper, inkier, like a damp fog. It clung to his skin. Even with the torch, he found himself stumbling in near blindness.

"Hey!" he shouted in the laughing, early stage of panic. His shout echoed. His voice was warped and elongated.

No reply.

He coughed, feeling the blackness in the back of his throat like cold smoke.

"Hey! This ain't funny (funny...funny...funny...)," his voice echoing, "I can't..." His foot hit a rock-hard object. He pitched forward, his face buried in the gypsum dust. Concho rose, eyes filled with the dust. He reached for the end of the torch. The light was barely visible though it was only inches away.

Spitting, drooling, gagging, feeling for the cave wall as he shouted for DeBack. The blackness closed around him like a soft chamber of moss, walls huddling in on him, ceiling and floor moving together. He was panting in thick, chilled air.

Dimly, as though across a bridge of centuries, he heard a faint voice. For a moment he stopped moving, stopped breathing, fearful that the wild pounding of his heart would obscure the distant cry.

He waited.

It came again. "Marco!"

Concho gasped for breath. "Polo!" he shouted back. (Polo...polo...polo...) "Marco Polo." The blind man's bluff game he'd played with his friends at a swimming hole, sometime in the past. How could DeBack have known?

Concho waited. Catching his breath.

"Mar-co!"

There. He knew the direction and began walking slowly, jerkily.

"Polo!"

Putting one foot carefully in front of the other. Easy does it.

"Marco!"

The voice grew stronger now.

One foot in front of the other. Stay calm.

"Polo!"

It was easier to get his breath.

"Marco!"

Concho could feel a breeze now. The air grew lighter, thinner. Faster he moved, running, stumbling.

"Are you a complete idiot?" DeBack asked calmly, silhouetted against the mouth of the cave.

Concho fell to the floor, wheezing, filling his lungs with fresh air, stretching, trying to shake off the feeling of horrible, damp suffocation.

"Don't go back there again," DeBack said, looming over him, taking away the torch, propping it up against a large rock near the entry of the cave.

"What's back there?"

DeBack helped Concho to a sitting position. "None of your business."

"Whaaa?" Concho panted, "What is it?"

"Ignorance is bliss."

"What is it?" Concho asked again, panting and pointing.

"The past, the future." DeBack jaw muscles flickered. His face looked heavy, sullen.

"The past...future?" Concho whispered, staring back into the darkness.

"Avoid it." DeBack stood and walked to the far side of the cave. He hefted a leather bag and dropped in the three apples.

Concho stood, leaning backward as if a wind was blowing him back toward the black rear of the cave.

DeBack eyed him steadily. "Hold on there, cowboy."

Concho shook his head, bewildered, rattled. "Come on, let's just have a peek. Check out some lottery numbers."

"Lottery number?"

"You know. Pick six. Win the big prize."

"Ah," DeBack said scornfully after a moment's pause. "Won't find any."

"It's worth a try."

DeBack swept his hand along the petroglyphs on the wall. "Do you see lottery numbers here? Baseball scores? Winning horses?"

Concho shrugged one shoulder.

"The big moments," DeBack said, shaking Concho's arm. "Major events, the march of history. Memories, and things to be. My scrapbook."

Concho's head tilted to one side, then slowly to the other, eyebrows jamming together, as he walked past near etchings. Crude sketches of faces, symbols and events—hundreds of them—he had seen in high school textbooks. Or was it in college? Some he recognized, others were unclear to him: Hitler, Abraham Lincoln, the American Eagle, Africans in slave ships, the steam engine, the French Revolution, martyrs burning at the Vatican, European monks in China, William the Conqueror slaughtering Britons, Nero in the midst of a burning Rome, the Cross of Jesus.

The finely carved glyphs stretched on and on, row on row, back to a single beginning at the mouth of the cave, a tableau a little larger than the others.

Framed in a delicate, filigree border was a tree bearing a rather good-looking snake, and a nude woman. To Concho's eye rather cravenly, explicitly depicted. A woman with substance in her shoulders, arms, legs, thighs, breasts, and a wedge of pubic hair delineated in startling detail. Firm, vigorous, a natural athlete. And all this off set by a face of perfect lovely innocence. A teenager's sense of adventure. A sturdy Iowa farm girl getting off the bus in L.A., ready for anything.

Farther off stood a man, looking lost, melancholy and a little dull. He was also naked, though drawn with less attention, with slack muscles, a poochy belly, an unenthusiastic penis looking like a misplaced thumb.

As Concho studied the glyph, he felt an unexpected tearing, choking sensation in his throat. His eyes began to fill with water and he quickly rubbed his face on his sleeve and cleared his throat.

He opened his eyes widely and blinked for a moment and realized that above this scene, unlike the other scenes, were etched some lines of poetry:

Of man's first disobedience, and the fruit
Of that forbidden tree whose moral taste
Brought death into the world, and all our woes.

"So this must be Eve," Concho said aloud, "and Adam and the snake."

He read the poetic lines again to himself.

"You write this?" Concho called over his shoulder.

"Yesss," a voice hissed in his ear.

Concho yelped and leapt forward, banging his head on the cave wall. "Ow!" he turned slightly and glared at DeBack. "Ow, Jesus...what'd you have to go sneaking up on me for?" He rubbed a bluish bulb growing on his forehead.

"That," said DeBack, in a flat voice, nodding at the poetic fragment, "is from *Paradise Lost*."

"Huh?" still stunned.

"The opening lines of *Paradise Lost*. Heard of it?"

"Oh, right. 'Course I have."

"Load of crap."

"Wait. You wrote it?"

DeBack glared at the writing. "Ever read it?"

Concho's mouth made a feint to one side. "Yeah, think so...everything's kinda cloudy."

A low growl. "It started out as a musical."

Concho eyed DeBack for a moment, his brow slowly wrinkling. "You sure?"

"It was going to be a collaboration. Like Gilbert and Sullivan. I even had a singing part. My voice is classically trained, you know. I was brilliant." DeBack stared hard at the wall, then gave a sharp exhalation of breath.

"What happened?"

"He went all traditional on me." DeBack shook all over, a flush coming to his face.

"Who did?"

"That damn Milton!" He turned to the cave's opening and stomped into the orangely-lit outdoors.

"What?" Concho called after him. "What happened?"

DeBack's eyebrows rose and fell. His lips were drawn into a crinkly, whitened tightness.

"It's in the past," he said. "All in the past."

Concho's head bobbed aimlessly and encouragingly. "Can't worry about the past."

"So they say."

"What's done is done."

"Mmm."

"Yep. You'll be starin' at the walls if the past's got you by the balls."

Concho grinned, his eyes bright. He nodded, glowing with the sort of dimwit pleasure cartoon characters experience just before an anvil drops out of the sky.

DeBack stared back. Beginning to tremble.

Concho grinned a little bit more.

"This is just not going to work," DeBack said slowly, staring beady-eyed at Concho with a look of illness, of nausea. He began fumbling furiously in a darkly stained leather bag.

"What?" Concho asked, blinking nervously.

Out of the bag DeBack pulled the three apples, gently laid them aside; a badger's skull, glanced at it, tossed it aside. Then a spark plug; a piece of cinnamon flavored gum; a bunch of chicken feathers tied together like a duster; a bluish rock the size of a baseball; a silvery, satin jacket; and a false eyelash.

The pile of objects lay scattered on the ground. He rummaged through them on hands and knees.

He was muttering to himself. Things like "ignoramus," and "For heaven sake." And "How'd I get myself into this?"

"What's wrong?"

DeBack's face snapped up, he stood and his iron fingers gripped Concho's neck.

"You! You're what's wrong!" he growled through locked molars. "Do you know what it takes to conjure up a guide? Do you know how long it takes? How many days?"

"Ngh," Concho couldn't breathe.

The fingers tightened. Concho's arteries stood out like copper tubing against his skin.

"I used my best stuff to conjure up a guide," DeBack barked. "And who do I get? Jed Clampet. Jed, friggin', Clampet."

Concho gave a dry, strangled reply, like a cat neutering itself jumping a picket fence. DeBack released him and immediately turned his attention back to the objects on the ground. After several minutes of moving them around, not finding what he was looking for, he scooped all but the badger skull back into the leather bag and slumped against the cave wall.

"Were you gonna un-conjure me?" Concho asked, alarmed, massaging his throat.

DeBack stared at him in hot anger. "It's not out of the question."

"Where would I go?"

DeBack shook his head. "Don't know. Probably to whatever little paradise you came from."

"I don't remember where I came from, 'cept that it's called Wisconsin."

"Click your heels together and see if that works." DeBack reclined back, stretching out. Tight-lipped. Brooding.

Concho shifted from one foot to the other in discomfort during the long, tense silence that followed, feeling like a house guest who caused the toilet to overflow. He wanted to go back to their friendlier conversation. His lips began to twitch and his eyeballs roved the walls.

"You make all them etchings?" he blurted.

DeBack's eyes glanced up. "Something like that." He brooded a little longer, then stared up at the drawing of Eve.

"You any relation to the one with the apple?" Concho asked, scrupulously eyeing the snake in the tree.

He sighed, wearily. "In a way."

"What kinda way? Great, great, great grandpa?"

Nope." DeBack shook his head, stared for a moment and made a decision.. "It's me."

Concho stared at him, waiting for this bit of information to find a toehold in his brain. "Y-you? This is you?"

"Yes."

Concho shook his head.

A bolt of lightning just outside the cave made them both jump.

DeBack cast a baleful look upward. "God, I hate lightning."

"With good reason, I'm sure."

"Hey, don't believe everything you read. I got suckered."

Concho had snuggled up against two large rocks, hands clasp behind his head, legs outstretched, crossed at the ankles. "How'd you get suckered?"

"It's too long a story."

Concho waved at the cave opening raging now with wind and slashing rain. "Don't think we're going anywhere anytime soon."

"You wouldn't believe me anyway."

"Hell, after what I've seen today, I'd believe just about anything. Snake asks me to get him some pruny apples. Then turns into a man...."

"Good point." DeBack gazed at the drawing. "Sometimes I don't believe it myself."

Concho started to speak, then stopped. DeBack's eyes had gone all funny. After a bit he seemed to recapture himself.

"You have to understand that, while the basic story is true, there are one or two important elements missing from the Biblical version."

"Such as?"

DeBack glared at Concho. "You want me to tell it or not?"

"Sorry."

DeBack tapped his pursed lips. "See, the Garden was pretty much as written about, except for one thing. We were still spirits, not quite finished with our shapes yet. I think that God was still trying to decide some of the final details when Satan..."

"The Devil?"

"Yes. When Satan—God's favorite angel—comes up to me and says that God wants the folks—that's what he calls Adam and Eve—to eat from the Tree of Knowledge, but he can't tell them himself because of some cosmic law regarding free will, but if I get them to do it for him, it'll be okay."

"And you fell for that?"

DeBack gave him a heavy-lidded, worldly-wise gaze. "Of course I fell for it. Remember, the world was extremely new. Nobody knew about good or evil, we were making it up as we went along."

"Yeah, but that's pretty transparent."

"Eden was a very transparent place. I did what I was told."

"You and the Nazis...."

"Hey, if you knew what you were talking about...."

"Maybe I don't." Concho straightened his reclined position. "But if you had been a little less gullible, maybe we'd all still be lounging around in Eden."

"But that's the point, if you'd let me finish." DeBack reached out his hand to where a small trickle of water dripped from the high ceiling. He let it pool in his palm, then wet his lips. "Ah. You see, God truly didn't know how to finish things up. Or maybe he recognized that there were things that could only be discovered by letting us find them out—whatever. All I know is that El Diablo did a good job conning me into taking a piece of fruit from the Tree of Life...."

"Tree of Life? I thought you said Tree of Knowledge."

DeBack stared at him for a moment. "Don't they read the Book of Genesis in Wisconsin?"

"Yeah, but I don't remember hearing about any other tree."

Half-wheeze, half sigh, DeBack sounded like the air had left his body. He shook his head.

"In the beginning, everything glimmered and shimmered—new. The mountains were like chocolate sundaes, rivers screamed with fish—silver and blue like have never been seen since. Trees were soft like broccoli." DeBack's face was soft, wistful. "Concho, old cheese, remember that even time had *just* begun. Time is the great toughener. We are born soft and die hard.

"Well, the world was born soft. The humans had just taken on their bodies, spirits wearing soft, new flesh. And the ideas; thought had only just been injected into this soft new place. It was like a drug—all this newness. The clouds sparkled, waiting to be given permission to rain. Everything was bright, pink and green and blue. Hells bells, the colors were all new, they'd just been invented."

He stopped, out of breath and glanced out toward the storm.

"That first rainbow didn't need rain to become. It was as if all the colors got together to celebrate their existence." He jumped up. "That was it! The world was celebrating its very birth. Sure I was gullible. The whole universe was giddy with existence."

"So the devil, Satan, comes up to you—surely he must have stuck out a little, with all the fresh beauty."

"No, no, no. It wasn't that simple." He scratched his head, gazed at the petroglyph. "Even evil was new. We were all so much in love with being alive. It was magnificent."

"Evil was new?"

"Yeah, we were all like teenagers roving around a brand new town. We were full of laughter, drunk with feeling—playfully immortal."

"Playfully?"

"Yeah, like kids. There were no rules. Well, one."

"Don't eat the fruit from the Tree of Knowledge?"

"Something like that."

"And you had to go and break it."

DeBack glared at Concho. "You keep forgetting that the world was new, busting at the seams with energy, brightness. Everything was amazing, everything was possible. Like the first time you go to a carnival."

"So, Satan walks up to you and says, 'DeBack, God just asked me to tell you to talk the woman into eating from the Tree of Knowledge. He was in too much of a hurry to tell you himself, so he sent me.' That's what happened?"

DeBack stared at the wall. "Sort of."

"Sort of?"

He turned red. "Actually, it was a bet with a little bit of a dare thrown in."

"You're kidding me. You gotta be pulling my leg."

DeBack stayed silent, chewing the inside of one lip.

Concho gasped. "Mankind is saddled with this *original sin* thing because of a bet with a little bit of a dare thrown in?"

"Sin had to start somewhere." DeBack shrugged. "Evil was new. I know it looks bad now, but it was a prank. I'm sure Satan thought God would laugh." A frown was visible on DeBack face. "Come to think of it, maybe he knew God wouldn't laugh. He was jealous of me! That it! He was jealous because I was more beautiful than any of God's creatures."

Concho's eyes took on a wide, staring gaze. "You...are...a...slithering idiot."

"Perhaps. Perhaps." His eyes went to that funny place again, came back with a smile that twisted slowly into a grimace. "And while sometimes I think the price, the punishment has been unfair or harsh....It was magnificent, being part of the beginning of all this."

His gaze swept the thousands of historic scenes.

They sat quiet for several minutes. As much as Concho wanted to know more, DeBack had gone to such a private place within himself, he didn't dare break the man's reverie. Shortly DeBack started tracing a design in the floor with his finger.

"DeBack, couldn't you have just told God what happened?"

"He wouldn't have listened."

"But you said everything was new—he might've laughed."

"Well, he didn't laugh. It was the biggest non-laugh ever."

"What happened?"

"The Ice Age."

Concho whistled, astonished.

"You forget, I lived through that, too." DeBack closed his eyes and let out a soft groan. "Do you have any idea what ice is like for a snake? Miles of it? Icy windswept wastes."

"Can't be that bad."

"Try crawling across Greenland sometime—naked."

"Sounds cool."

DeBack laughed bitterly. "Cool? No. It gave a whole new meaning to being cold-blooded."

"The ice age? Aw, had to be fun, all those woolly mammoths."

DeBack rubbed his shoulder. "Couldn't see where they were walking with all that hair."

Concho squinted. One end of his mouth gave a wavering, uncertain smile.

"Next time you've got about forty thousand years to kill," DeBack said, "spend it in someone's deep freeze. People complain about the world now, but they can't even guess what the Ice Age was like. Least now there's central heating."

"Can't guess?"

"Yeah. Most people comprehend nothing of the past. Me on the other hand, I have no choice, I'm spread out there every day in every century."

Concho's nose twitched and he gazed off into the middle distance, hoping to convey a sense of profound comprehension.

"You don't get any of this do you," DeBack said.

"Well...."

"Never mind." DeBack settled down on the floor, preparing for sleep.

"Oh come on. Get it off your chest."

"You wouldn't understand."

"Why not?"

"Because you're...you're..."

"What? I'm what?"

DeBack shook his head and sighed, a reptile acquainted with futility. "Okay. You won't understand this. I'm wasting my breath. It'll probably give you a migraine just trying to process it."

"Spit it out, you, you dumb snake."

"All right." DeBack held up his hands. "The past, present and future exist simultaneously." He took a breath. "Most people, mammals, invertebrates, et cetera, get reincarnated. Means they build up memories. Means they live simultaneously in all kinds of decades. But best of all, it means they get a breather between lives. Like that space between songs on a CD."

"On CDs?"

DeBack waved it off. "Have you heard anything I've said?"

"Course I did. Most mammals get a breather between lives," he said, then asked, "And you don't?"

"No. God, no, it's been straight through. I'm out there somewhere in the world every day. Every second. Every damn decade. I'm spread pretty thin."

Concho rubbed a tight spot in the center of his forehead.

"What's the matter?" DeBack asked.

"Giving me a headache."

'That's because your conscious mind is pounding up against the sixth wall."

Concho stared at DeBack for a long, long time, then he laid down, curled up into a fetal position. "I don't think I wanna know any more."

"I warned you."

Concho shook his head. "It's been the longest day of my life."

DeBack smiled. "I doubt it. Wait awhile."

The two settled into comfortable positions and began to drift toward sleep. The rain chattered outside. DeBack's breath grew low and deep.

Concho stirred once and in a groggy voice asked, "DeBack?"

DeBack grunted.

"DeBack, why'd you conjure me up?"

For a moment all Concho heard was a deep, steady breathing. Then DeBack licked his lips and turned on his side.

"What?"

"Why'd you conjure me?"

After another long, somnolent pause, DeBack mumbled sleepily, "Because I need you."

"What can I possibly do to help you?" he raised up on one elbow, rolling slightly to look at the snake man.

"Sorry, old bub. I'm just too tired to..."

"Too tired to do what?"

"To save the world all by myself." DeBack rolled over, blinked twice and ran his tongue along the slight smile on his lips before he slept.

♌♌♌

She turned her head at the sound of a fist slamming against the wooden table. Mugs bounced and beer spilled. She grabbed a towel from the bar and hurried toward him.

"E pluribus factotum!" He roared, waving his hands around. "That bloody, bloody snake."

"Master Milton," she said, creating a cloth dam to catch the spilled beer. "You know what happens every time you start spraying that Latin around the room."

"He's doing it again." Milton waved toward her voice, his sightless eyes scrunched as if it would help him locate her. "I can feel that bastard taking false credit for my efforts."

"Shh. What bastard?"

"That snake of a man. That busker." His searching hand found her sleeve, pulled her closer. "He wanted to turn my *Paradise Lost* into a musical, with him playing the lead. Can you imagine, Annie?"

"No, I can't sire." She gently extricated herself from his grasp, started to the bar to wring out the beer-soaked rag.

"That bastard. *Maledictus non apropris.*"

As if on cue, the constable pushed through the door, walked over to the blind poet and lifted him by his collar.

"Come along now, sire. Your room is ready for you."

Milton flailed. "How dare you! Hands off, you Protestant!"

Annie sighed. T'was the same every time. The normally quiet, genteel poet would fly into this snake rage, the constable would arrive, throw him into the hoosegow overnight. He'd be back tomorrow with an outrageous tale of his latest cell mate. The last one was a grossly overweight poacher, named Illford, who had a violent case of inflamed bowels.

Poets or poachers, all men were pigs.

Off in the distance she thought she could hear the sound of a split-tongue laughter.

"Annie. Angel." Someone was calling her. "Angel. Mrs. Williams. Wake up."

She sat up, looked around. Blinked. Nothing but metal and lights. She shook her head to clear the image.

More metal.

"Where am I?" she growled.

"Cyrus One." The voice seemed to come right out of the wall.

"My name is Cyrus?"

"Your name is Angel. Cyrus One is the federal space station."

"I'm an angel? Already?"

"You are Angel Williams," the voice said without exasperation, or any other emotion. "The wife of the vice president of the United States. Remember?"

Angel nodded, hating to give up the warm, smoky dream. She rubbed her eyes let her hands drift down her body. She had liked being the busty barmaid, resented her sleek, greyhound shape. Not enough bumps.

"Where am I?"

"Space."

She jumped off the metal bed and walked over to the porthole. Oh yeah. Eight hundred miles out in space. She and the Cyrus One Federal Space Station were held in a fixed position over Washington, D.C., as if by a slender thread. While the Earth spun around the sun.

The station, shaped like a giant hamster wheel, rolled lazily in a counter clockwise direction, creating an even, comfortable, OSHA-approved gravity field inside.

And she was one of the hamsters.

She pressed her nose against the porthole, let her eyes gaze along the exterior which jutted here and there with gadgetry and hoses and very expensive nozzles, and was covered in a skin of white protective ceramic tiles—like a huge bathroom turned inside out.

American flags, Eagles and Latin phrases were placed at patriotic intervals around the ship, so that no matter what direction it might be seen, the C1FSS boasted its ingenious American origin.

"E pluribus ad nauseam..." she muttered, knowing it was partly her own fault.

The publicity shots seen on the evening news back on Earth showed a serene, gloriously white government complex, floating against the somber backdrop of space. The very symbol of the American empire.

To the people of Earth, Cyrus One represented solemnity, dignity and scrappy American-can-doism at work.

Images that would keep a president in office for another term—another year, a few months, a few weeks—just long enough...

President Panic's image was silhouetted on the video screen against a blue background, flanked by flags. "We're working on solutions for the future. Americans need not live in fear."

It was a great plan, except Panic had refused to leave his cubicle for weeks now, forcing the engineers to alter the message digitally each day to effect slight variations. The broadcast had worked well at first, his approval rating climbing a point or two each time the avuncular message was microwaved to earth.

Now the technical magic was wearing thin. The public began to clamor for a live news conference despite the fact that reporters were not allowed in space. Voters clamored to know why the government had moved to C1FSS, why the executive wing of the government had picked up, packed up, and moved into outer space? There were problems that needed to be solved on terra firma. Americans needed to see their president on the green, green grass of home. In fact, a contingent of junior congressmen who'd been left on earth, led by California Rep. Jim Carrey, began using the "I" word.

Impeachment.

A series of ads with comforting scenes of rural roads at sunrise and babies being joyfully tossed in the air with a Hal Rinney voice-over were being prepared, but optimism on board C1FSS was not running high. The ads had not tested well in Seattle or in Atlanta. If the president was impeached, many of those now in safety might be returned to the planet's surface.

This would not do.

Speech writers mopped their brows; spin doctors conjured up other images. The interior of C1FSS was chaos. Loud epithets flew out office doors. Piles of trash littered the metal hallways. Toilets were backing up beyond the ability of the engineers to "go with the flow."

And worst of all they were nearly out of alcohol.

In desperation, a deal was struck with the Oprah Rivera Springer people. O.R.S. could visit the space station, do a little taping, and ask no more than five pre-approved questions if—and here was the catch—she/he would bring a shipping carton of Jack Daniels, Russian vodka, Cuervo Gold, marguerita mix and a selection of California wines.

Angel tapped her fingers against the thick plexiglass porthole as if trying to move the clouds from between her and Earth's surface. She fought to bring back the dream-life she'd been living when awakened. The feel of low-cut cotton against her shoulders, the swish of a full dress around her hips and legs, the laughter of men bouncing off wood and stone.

The door whooshed open and she turned.

"What do you want?"

He wore the smile he'd used to seduce her in hundreds of different ways over the past ten years.

"I'm here to grant you your wish."

"Gee, a fairy god husband. Who'd have thunk."

"Funny." The smile only flickered. He'd been a politician too long. "And they wonder why I love you so much."

"Do you?"

"I love being vice president, and you helped make that happen."

She turned back toward the porthole. "Let's not get too gushy."

He laughed. "The shuttle will be here tomorrow and you can leave with it the day after. Unless you change your mind. I'll be back tonight to visit with you."

She nodded.

After a moment the whoosh told her he was gone. She turned, wiping the tears from her cheek.

"I won't."

♌♌♌

Concho continued to hover over DeBack.

The storm had cleared, and outside the cave hard, white, morning sunlight turned the landscape into a wide, spacious, Texas-size frying pan.

DeBack snorted once and opened his eyes.

"When you say 'Save the world,' you do mean metaphorically, right?" Concho asked.

DeBack rubbed his face and sat up. "No."

Concho swallowed hard.

"I'm so hungry," DeBack yawned, rising and stretching. He poked his head behind a rock that jutted at an angle from the cave wall. "Yes. Thought I had something saved up back here."

He stuck his arm up to his shoulder behind the rock, feeling around, holding his tongue to one side and retrieved a dark, matted lump. A dead rat.

"Ah, rattatooie." He smiled, letting the creature dangle by its long, stiff tail. "Care for a bite?"

"No thanks," Concho said.

"Now, I'd just bet that somewhere back in one of your lifetimes you've eaten a rat before."

Concho felt himself becoming sick. "That may be. But I'm guessing the whole point of western civilization has been to find ways not to."

"Touché."

DeBack held the rat over his mouth and in a single gulp devoured it. He smacked his lips tastily, patted his belly and burped with gusto. "Breakfast of champions."

"Let's get back to this saving-the-world business," Concho said, whose hunger had dissolved after DeBack's long gulp.

"Ah."

DeBack strode out of the cave and stood in the harsh sunlight, shading his eyes.

"Let me see," he said, gazing around. "The sun is coming from the east, so..." He pivoted a quarter turn to the right and pointed into the blue southern sky. "There."

"What?" Concho asked, his eyes slowly growing accustomed to the brilliant light.

"Over there—somewhere." DeBack waved his finger around.

"Where exactly?"

"There." He waved vaguely. "What do you see?"

"Nothing."

"Really?"

Concho shook his head. "Blue sky."

DeBack headed back into the cave. "Hang on," he called out and began digging through the leather bag. He emerged moments later with a huge, showy, false eyelash.

"Put this on."

"Oh, come on."

He shook it at him. "Put the damn thing on."

Concho grimly accepted the eyelash and held it up to one of his eyes. The wrong way.

"No, no, no," DeBack chided. "Didn't your mother ever wear these things"

"I don't recall ever having a mother. Much less her wearing something like that."

"Okay, here we go."

DeBack licked the backing on the eyelash and stuck it to Concho's eyelid. "Just keep it closed for a few seconds. Let it adhere."

As he stood there waiting for the thing to stick, Concho realized that somewhere he probably had friends or relatives who would be highly suspicious of a story about him walking through this West Texas desert landscape with a naked man who later asked him to wear a false eyelash.

"Okay, now just open the eye with the false eyelash," DeBack said.

Concho hefted the one eyelid up. It felt heavy and awkward. He concentrated on the sky, staring into the vast blueness, squinting, focusing until the blue of the sky seemed to draw closer to him, until it felt he might slip and fall headlong into the infinite blueness. Slowly, it was broken up by tiny chips of light and as he watched something began to move through the vast backdrop. A DARK thing, a moving, hurtling thing.

"What is it?" he asked, numb, a terrible sensation of a calamity tying his guts in a knot.

"That's it," DeBack announced and turned back toward the cave humming a tune from *Bridge Over the River Kwai.*

"We're going to save the world from that?"

Concho tugged off the eyelash and followed him inside.

"What is it?" he asked, handing the eyelash to DeBack.

DeBack accepted the eyelash, slipped it back into the bag. He glanced up at Concho, a sad smile on his face.

"What is it?"

DeBack hoisted the bag over one shoulder and made his way out of the cave, "That, my good friend, is the future, headed right for us."

♌♌♌

Leah squatted down, pushed a stray hair back from her face, sought a puff of breeze off the nearby water. There was none. No wonder they call it the Dead Sea. She smiled, looked around. This was perfect, the absolute silence, the absolute heat and emptiness. No noise, no boys. Another grin. Archeology had become the perfect getaway. No arguments. A holy task.

She glanced up into the empty blue sky. Somewhere up there her mother and father were floating like a pair of Cheerios in the Milky Way.

Earth was better. Israel better still. She reached for the clay water jug and moved the soft-bristle tooth brush against it with care, humming a tune she'd heard from Saleem the last night they spent together. Someday she'd ask him the words, if there were any.

Maybe she'd just stay here, go from dig to dig for say...another forty years. That'd do it. Her own little piece of sandy heaven.

She turned the jug over to scour the base. A curled piece of ancient, gray sheep's skin slipped out onto the ground between her feet.

She blinked at it, then carefully, with the tip of the brush, she turned the hide over to reveal a fragment of text, strokes of a reed dipped in faded vegetable ink.

She pulled the hair away from her eyes, tucked it behind her ears and bent over the fragment, fearful that her very breath might cause it to disintegrate into dust. Sweat glistened on her face and neck. Her lips tightened and she swallowed nervously several times. This was the real thing, a piece of an ancient scroll. Her heart beat faster.

With dizzy, disbelieving eyes she tried to read the primitive Hebrew writing, left to right. Her eyes passed back and forth over it, concentrating with her spare knowledge of the language, but the words kept their secret meaning from her.

Feeling faint and disoriented, Leah drew away and called out the name of Dr. Pitters, the dig master.

She found him in the central tent bent over a table.

"Dr. Pitters."

He waved her quiet. She walked around to see what he was examining.

It was a tea cup.

"Dr. Pitters, I've found a..."

"Quiet, I'm almost through."

He made several markings on a pad of paper, took one last look in the cup, then leaned back and rubbed his eyes.

"The future's far more difficult to discover than the past," he said, dumping the tea leaves from the cup. "According to this, the light of real knowing will soon be upon us."

Leah leaned forward. "But that's what I've come to show you."

"Eh?"

She proffered the jar. "In here, take a look at this."

Pitters took the jar. "A good specimen."

"Inside. Inside."

He extracted the ancient sheep skin, a bit of vellum. A swarm of small stinging gnats invaded the air about his eyes. He took no notice.

"Can you read it?" Leah asked, leaning over his shoulder.

Pitters licked his lips and adjusted his finger-printed glasses, wiping his hand down a graying beard that was thick with yellowish dust. The sweat trickled out of his hair cutting small channels in the dust, running into the lines of his deep cragged face.

"Dr. Pitters."

"Yes. Yes, I can read it."

She put her hand on his shoulder. "What does it say?"

Pitters rubbed his beard with the back of his hands. Rubbed it first one direction, then another. He gazed at the fragment, closed his eyes.

Leah straightened up. "What's it say?"

He shook his head. "If I'm reading this right, the universe was started by accident. Like an unwanted pregnancy."

"But that's not what Genesis..."

Again that dismissing wave.

With the palm of a wooden thong, he lifted the scrap of text into a hinged wooden box. After he'd laid it carefully inside, he closed the box and snapped its lock.

"Is this the urn you were cleaning?" he asked, lifting the slim clay pot.

She nodded.

Pitters put his eye to the narrow mouth of the vessel. He held it back, to allow some light inside. Several times he gently shook the pot.

"What?" the girl asked, leaning forward.

"Well," Pitters said, his eye again at the lip of the opening. "Seems to be another one inside."

"Another vellum?"

"Appears so," he murmured, his voice beginning to glow with excitement, "we'll have to break it open. See what's written on it."

"But I spent over three days cleaning it."

Pitters turned with a smile. "And the world has waited thousands of years to hear what it has to say."

♌♌♌

Concho and DeBack had walked for most of the morning through scrubby flatland under the bombardment of a sweltering, anger-oriented sun that had already dried out the surface of West Texas. Concho wiped his neck with a bandanna and almost began to wish he'd taken a nibble of that rat. His mouth was dry, his head felt light. He needed food and a cold drink.

They crossed a two-lane highway, and sat in the shade of a large billboard. Each time a car whizzed by, about one every half-hour, they stuck out their thumbs. Time passed. More time passed. More time passed than cars.

It was noon. Not a cloud in the sky. And the shade of the billboard had reduced itself to a strip the thickness of the sign.

"Thought you said we wasn't gonna have good weather," Concho said, with a sigh.

DeBack looked at the cloudless sky as if he hadn't noticed.

"We're two thousand miles from Washington." Concho wailed. "How the hell're we gonna get there?"

"Trust me," DeBack said.

"Ha!" he replied in a dry, hoarse voice. "The snake of snakes says 'trust me'. That's a good one."

♌♌♌

Clifford Clemp pressed his small, sputtering mouth against the silvery screen of the large microphone, "And when it arrives," he growled, "the weather's gonna change, oh yes, and there'll be earthquakes and tidal waves and hurricanes and pestilences and famine and sudden destruction!"

He grabbed up a rusted sheet of roofing tin and vigorously shook it.

"And nation shall rise against nation," he shouted above the artificial thunder, "and the whole world shall be a field of desolation and woe unto the inhabitants of the earth who will gnash their teeth and cry for the rocks and mountains to fall upon them. For in that day, the Lord of Hosts will smite them with furious..."

A loud clack.

Clifford let out a woof of surprise, lurching in his swivel chair, glancing around the small home-built studio for the source of the interruption.

Rivers of black wire cascaded down the walls and swirled in wild eddies at his feet. A large panel blinked furiously, with sound-level needles swinging back and forth like slashing knives.

"Dagnabit," Clifford muttered.

It was the reel-to-reel again. A Nixon-era device that was given to shutting off in mid-taping. He pressed his heels against the floor, pushing the chair over the corduroy of wires, bumping, jostling his chubby, boyish face.

With a pained expression, he punched the rewind button, letting the tape spool backward a few seconds.

"...ay, the Lord of Host will smite them with furious..."

He listened to the sound of his voice with wry dissatisfaction. Never liked the sound of it. A bit too much eeking out of the nose, a voice given to shrillness, whiney intonation, that back-of-the-palate flatness in mid-range. But there was a bright side. He'd nearly saved up enough for another elocution lesson with Miss Berry in Abilene. He needed more lessons. He smiled to himself at the thought of sitting in Miss Berry's dark front room, surrounded by Turkish rugs and Queen Anne furniture, or sipping mint tea with her in the afternoon. She had promised a generous sum to Clemp's ministry when the Lord called her to live with Him in that Home Beyond the Blue. And in the meantime when he could scare up the $25 per lesson, she would teach him the hidden techniques of diction, breathing and good speaking.

He flipped the off switch on the reel-to-reel. It needed to cool off. So did he. The day promised to be a hot one and it was that once-a-year time for tidying up his scattered billboards.

The white light on the studio telephone began to flash. From faraway in another part of the rectory, he could hear his other phone ringing.

"Notre Dung," he said.

"Clifford," his mother rasped. "I had the dream again."

"Mom."

"You were there, Clifford, you were there!"

"Mom, please."

"They was listening to you. All them bigwigs, they was hanging on your every word."

"Was I wearing the..."

"Yes! Yes! It was beautiful, the lights gleaming off of it. Bouncing off like diamonds. And Clifford—they was hearing you. All them high muckety-mucks."

"Was Dick Cavett there?"

"He was there! And so was Ed McMahon and Donald Trump with his wife and that fella from 20/20."

"Hugh Downs?"

"Yes! He was there too and so was Daisy Fuentes."

"Who?"

"Daisy Fuentes. From, oh, you know. She's on CNBC. Got a talk show or something."

"Oh."

"Pretty Mexican gal."

"I must have missed that one."

"Clifford, this ain't just a dream," she said. "Ain't just some flight of fancy. I'm telling you, this is real. It's *real!* I could smell the food, I could feel the thick, white table cloths. I could see the view of New York City spread out for miles."

"The Rainbow Room?"

"You were there. You were there."

"Rockefeller Center?"

"The Lord has a work for you, Clifford—and it ain't rabbit manure. It ain't. And you know it."

"Rabbit pellets have been good to me, Mom," he said softly. "Very good fertilizer. Gardeners love it. And visitors pay to see it."

"Clifford, your father was a joke and now you're becoming a joke. Who ever heard of a church being built from rabbit s-s-h-i, uh, rabbit poop?" She never could bring herself to say the word she wanted to say. "God's house! Built from rabbit poop. Disgusting."

Clifford's mouth shrank, his eyes hardened. They had gone over this a hundred times before.

"Mother. The Lord works in mysterious ways His wonders to perform."

"Well, my boy, you ain't never gonna convince me that the spirit of the Almighty would ever consider making his dwelling place near that pile of rabbit pills."

"Yes, I think you mentioned that a time or two."

"And I'll say it again. And I'll keep on saying it until you see that you're cut from a finer cloth. You're headed for something bigger than you've dared to dream."

"Thanks, Mom."

A pause. The voice grew soft. "You were there, Clifford."

"Okay, okay. I was there. Wearing the jacket. Warning of the end of the world. Thanks."

Clifford clamped down the phone and paced around the tiny studio. He didn't need this pressure on top of everything else he had going. He kicked at the swivel chair and bustled out of the room. He needed air, needed to think.

His home, the rectory, was a slanted shanty that had been losing its layer of paint for more than two decades. The roof sagged a bit in the middle. The front porch looked like it had been stolen from another house. A nicer house.

To the side of the rectory loomed a profoundly large mountain of graying rabbit manure. A wide, empty parking lot stretched out in front of the rectory, a large rabbit-shaped sign cheerfully welcomed the horde of visitors who were not there.

The giant hill of rabbit manure was a local attraction. Had been for some 30 years, a year or so after his father had bought five pair of white rabbits. He remembered working hard cleaning up after them for his dad, when he was still alive, and building God's mountain. The fast-multiplying animals and their poop had built the pews, an altar, and had even paid for the church building, the odd site known as, "Notre Dung."

Tourists for two hundred fifty miles in either direction were challenged by large, unattractive highway signs such as:

"Don't Miss the World's Largest Heap of Rabbit Droppings.'" or, "250 mi. to the World's Largest Pile of Rabbit Pills," or, "Hey! You Just Passed the Planet's Biggest Mound of Rabbit Poop."

The fact that the *heap of rabbit droppings* was also a religious site was saved until the unsuspecting, unbelieving tourist drove up and paid their entrance fees.

"Catching souls is a lot like killing flies," the senior Clemp had often been heard to say. "You gotta get 'em at the last minute. When they least expect it."

So, for decades, when the interstate was the lifeblood of family vacations, Notre Dung had succeeded in a big way.

Clifford Clemp stood on the porch of the faded shanty and surveyed the emptiness of the parking lot. Some speck of his brain ruminated on the metaphorical similarities between the parking lot and his love life. But the part of his brain dedicated to such introspection had been locked in a steel box and dropped into the dank waters of his lower cortex.

The part of Clifford's brain that functioned outside of the locked box glared at the carless, visitorless parking lot and cursed mildly.

Sex and television. That's all people had time for these days. Any disposable income folks had this year was going to mail-order love toys or to HBO. Not much was going into the roadside attraction industry.

Well, sex and television be damned! There was still work to be done in this country.

Muttering, he hulked into the barn across the paved country road behind the rectory and spent the next twenty minutes preparing his biplane, a World War I relic. He loaded cans of exterior paint into the empty passenger seat.

"So much emptiness!" cried a voice within his head.

Clifford looked about, startled. From his back pocket, he took out a tarnished silver hip flask, whisked off the top and took a deep, satisfying gulp.

He glanced at his watch. Nothing better at 10 a.m. He took another gulp and emptied the flask. Belched. Shook the flask and a single drop whipped around inside. He tipped it up one last time and drank the final drip.

"Empty like your love," the voice said.

Clifford glanced around as he replaced the flask's top.

He kicked the blocks out from under the plane's wheels, took hold of the tow line and straining, grunting and swearing, he wheeled the plane out onto the empty country road.

He spun the prop and the engine gave a cough and stopped. A puff of white smoke shot out of the exhaust. Clifford reached up his full length, wrapped his fingertips around the edge of the prop and gave it another hard spin.

Cough. Putt. Cough. Putt, putt. Cough, cough. Putt, putt, putt, putt...

The prop began to spin and Clifford hurdled his round self onto the wing and into the pilot's seat, dropped goggles over his face and steered the plane down the two-lane road. He groped around on the floorboard until he found a three-quarters empty bottle of Old Tennessee. He pulled off the cap with his teeth, chug-a-lugged the rest and hurled the empty over the side.

The plane rolled bumpily down the road and slowly rose into the air. Clifford made one low pass over the world's largest pile of rabbit pellets, then soared into the azure Texas sky, heading west-southwest.

♌♌♌

"Concho!"

"What?"

"Duck!"

DeBack yanked Concho to the ground, seconds before being turned into human linguine by Clifford Clemp's low swooping biplane.

The plane continued its quick descent, taxiing down the blacktop roadway, sending up flurries of debris on either side of the road. A half mile down the road Concho saw a sudden whirl of dirt on the shoulder where a car swerved to miss hitting the plane. He watched as the miniature figure in the car burst from the driver's side and performed a dance of angry gestures.

The plane then turned around and headed for the arm-waving driver, who hesitated, shook a fist, hesitated again and leaped back into the car. Weaving from side to side, he sped toward Concho and DeBack, finally whooshing past them in a dark blur. A sports car. A flash.

"Did you see that?" Concho asked.

DeBack nodded.

"Holy Mother Tabasco!" Concho fumed. "Who the hell does that pilot think he is?"

The plane jostled back up the two-lane highway and came to a stop near the billboard.

The pilot hopped out. A rotund, red-faced man. He tore off his goggles, mopped his broad sunburnt forehead with a rag and squinted at the two.

"Howdy," Concho said with a quick wave to the pilot.

With his fat tongue emerging to lick sweat off his upper lip, the aviator stared first at Concho then at DeBack. He studied DeBack longer, with a mix of perplexity and half-recognition.

"Hello there," he said at last, rubbing both hands with a rag, then stuffing it into a back pocket. "I'm afraid I gotta ask you boys to give up your shade. Gotta spruce this thing up a little." Indicating the billboard.

Clemp turned toward the plane again, climbed up on the wing and retrieved two five-gallon buckets of paint from the back passenger seat. He hopped down with sunny, chubby enthusiasm, stumped over to the base of the large sign and dropped the paint with a theatrical grunt.

With another grunt he leaned far back, looking up, checking the billboard.

"Only 250 miles to the World's Biggest Pile of Rabbit Manure." it said in panels of chipped and peeling red exterior paint.

DeBack looked uneasily at Concho, then jerked his head toward the biplane. Concho's forehead made a questioning expression. DeBack gave his eyes an exasperated roll, nodded once with upraised eyebrows in a way that meant, *pay attention,* and then spasmed his head toward the biplane.

Concho shrugged, completely lost.

DeBack turned around and silently shook his fist at the sky.

"You boys know God?" Clemp asked, ever the evangelist, as he sat down on one of the large buckets, and rolled from one buttock to the other on the furled edge of the lid.

"He does," Concho blurted, jerking a thumb in DeBack's direction.

"Really?" Clemp smiled, looking at DeBack in a new light.

DeBack, turning back around, nodded, bringing a tight sneer to his face.

"Nothing like it," Clemp said. "Nothing like a walk with your creator."

"Yesss," DeBack replied with an involuntary hiss. For a moment his lips took on a reptilian thin whiteness, his eyes going to black beady slits, even his skin appearing, for an instant, to have the fragmentation of a snake. The effect lasted only a second. DeBack cleared his throat and it seemed to have been a trick of the light.

Even so, Clemp gave a start, his mouth coming open.

"We're trying to hitch a ride," Concho fairly shouted. Placing himself between Clemp and DeBack.

Clemp leaned around Concho, searching DeBack's face again, finding only a placid smile and an affable demeanor.

"Where yuh headed?" Clemp asked, turning to Concho, but keeping an eye on DeBack with subtle sideway glances.

"Washington, D.C."

"Got a long way to go," Clemp said. "Lucky for you gents the Greyhound outa El Paso comes right by here."

"You hear that?" Concho said to DeBack.

"Yeah, I bet if you flagged 'em down you'd get a ride," Clemp added.

Concho noticed that DeBack was suddenly rummaging around in his leather bag.

"Flag 'em down you say?" DeBack called out, his head inside the bag.

"Mmm-humm," Clemp said.

"With what?"

"Oh, I don't know, maybe a shirt or a..."

"Something like this?"

DeBack held aloft a bunch of chicken feathers bound together with a thin leather string. At first they hung motionless in the still, dead air. Then slowly they began to stir. First one, then a second, then the whole bunch moving like beckoning fingers.

Clemp's forehead creased as he watched the feathers move as though stirred by a breeze.

"Yes, this might flag them down," DeBack said in a velvety tone, his eyebrows arching, his pupils going to tiny, cold-blooded dots. "Waving as they do back and forth, back and forth. Kinda makes you sleepy doesn't it, as they whisper back and forth, back and forth. Sort of dreamy how they rustle together, like heads of wheat, golden grain sweeping back and forth, back and forth, as if you're a child in a giant field of wheat, back and forth, back and forth, it's such a warm day and the smell of the wheat is rich and aromatic, back and forth, back and forth. You just want to lie down, lie down and sleep for just a little while, back and forth, back and forth, you're so sleepy and the sun is so warm that you..."

Thud.

DeBack glanced around to see Concho sprawled out unconscious and snoring at the edge of the road.

"I don't think you'll flag it down that way," Clifford Clemp said in a helpful, cherry voice. "You done put that guy to sleep. You got to put some elbow grease into it. Like this."

Clemp jumped his chubby self up, a foot on each bucket, and waved both arms like an aerobics instructor.

DeBack gave Concho a swift kick. "Wake up."

"Ugh?"

"Wake up, wake up."

Concho sat upright on the edge of the roadway and rubbed both sides of his face.

"Doncha got something else in there might work?" Clemp asked, hopping off the bucket, indicating DeBack's leather bag.

"No, I don't," DeBack grumbled.

"Well, I'm sure the Lord will provide something." Clemp said. "I know that whenever I've been in a fix, something always comes along."

"Like you said, the Greyhound should be coming along," DeBack said, kicking at a rock. The scrubby desert landscape all around was strewn with rocks and small, struggling plants.

"Though I walk through the valley of the shadow of death, I will fear no evil," Clemp quoted, bending and prying the lid off one of the cans of paint. The metal bent and squawked before breaking loose.

Concho and DeBack squatting at the edge of the asphalt, squinting into the cloudless Texas sky, watched heat waves shimmer off the road.

"You know, though," Clemp said, stirring the thick paint. "Seems if I'm not mistaken, it may not come by until early in the morning. Round six."

"The bus?" Concho asked, waking up at last.

"Yep."

"But I ain't had nothing to eat since yesterday. Maybe before."

"Wish I could help you," Clemp said. "I don't think I have anything in the plane."

"If you're really religious, you could turn these rocks into bread," DeBack said, his eyes closed, sunning himself dreamily.

"The answer to that is get thee behind me, Satan," Clemp responded, glaring at DeBack.

"Just a thought," DeBack replied.

"I don't think I exactly trust you," Clemp said.

"No reason you should," DeBack answered, leaning back, stretching out his long body.

Clemp climbed one leg onto the billboard's ledge. He stood on the creaky wooden border, looking down to Concho said, "Could you hand up that bucket of red?"

Concho moaned and ambled over to the paint, bent and lifted the large can up to Clemp's waiting hands.

"I got a lotta these guys to get cleaned up. Got these billboards scattered all over a 250 mile radius." He pulled out a brush, and began to repaint the sign, half-singing, half-humming, "There's a Fountain Filled With Blood."

"What were you up to?" Concho whispered to DeBack.

"With the chicken feathers?"

"Yeah."

"A little hypnotism," he said in a low guttural voice. "We need that plane."

"Oh, and you thought you could hypnotize him , and then what? Steal it?"

"Of course."

Concho shook his sweaty head. "We can wait for the bus if we have to."

"No, we can't. There's not enough time."

"Well," Concho began, "We could always make a run for it. He's up there on the sign. We're down here."

"No, no, no."

"You got any money?"

"Not on me. I have a couple Roman coins back in the cave but..."

"Why didn't you bring them?" Concho asked.

"Because they're keepsakes. They were pressed into Nero's eyes when he died."

"Why didn't you bring money?"

"I don't have any. I don't think," searching around in his pockets. He turned the empty pockets inside out. "Gosh darn, I don't want the world to end just cause you didn't think to scare up a little cash."

"I don't have any money!" DeBack snapped.

Concho fumed and threw up his arms, "Jesus!"

"What's that?" Clemp shouted down from the sign.

"Nothing, nothing," Concho said with a quick wave. He turned to DeBack. "Why don't you dump out that bag. Maybe we can trade him something."

"No way."

"Yes, way, gimme that." Concho lunged for the bag.

DeBack shifted it behind his back. "Don't you dare."

Concho looked at him, an air of defeat in his eyes. "Yeah, I guess you're right." He began to turn away—a feint—he flashed around and popped his shoulder into DeBack's gut sending the snake man and the bag flailing backward. For a moment they were airborne. A thick puff of choking dust erupted when the two men and the bag simultaneously hit the ground . Out of the dust cloud came grunts and angry cries and the scuffing of boots. The Bag was hurled away from the eruption of arms and legs, spilling out its contents one by one as it tumbled to a sudden stop.

Clemp watched the goings on with a mix of amusement and resignation. Two bums, he thought, fighting over scraps. And people wonder why there'll never be world peace.

A flash of silver hit Clemp's eyes, making him flinch, raising up his arms like Paul on the Road to Damascus who was struck down by the brilliance of God's presence.

The bag had unloosed its last item. A silvery jacket lay on top of the other items that had spilled free.

He froze, his eyes locked on the jacket. "It's just like in the dream," he said.

DeBack and Concho, panting and wiping dirt out of their eyes glanced up at Clemp, sensing the profound shift in the pilot's attention.

Clemp seemed to have stopped breathing. His whole body inched forward. His fingertips, wiggling involuntarily, dropped the paint brush. His mouth open emitting small wanting noises. The twitches and choked mewling of a REM dreamer.

He jumped down from the sign and began walking slowly toward the silvery gleam.

DeBack held his eyes on Clemp. He stood and gently picked up the jacket, raising it up with one dirty finger, moving it gently side to side, letting the brilliant midday sun cascade and shoot through the summit and valleys of the material. Tiny bursts of ruby and blue diamonds sprayed off the peaks of fabric. They formed then vanished as DeBack let the garment sway this way and that.

"It's a lovely thing," DeBack murmured, in a plush, hypnotic voice. "Very lovely, don't you think?"

"It's just like the dream," Clemp whispered, his eyeballs the size of deviled eggs. "May I hold it?"

"Absolutely," DeBack said.

With trembling hands Clemp took the jacket and sat down on one of the paint containers. Over and over he stroked the fabric, letting the jacket lay across his lap. His fingers exploring the tucks and turns of the material, his eyes dazzled by the sparkle of it all.

"Try it on," DeBack purred.

Clemp's face scrunched up suddenly, and he made a sound so high-pitched it could barely be heard. Then he burst into tears and buried his face in the jacket.

"It's so beautiful," he sobbed over and over. "It's so beautiful."

He wept without embarrassment, rocking back and forth, holding the jacket close to his body. How many nights had he lain on his lonely army-cot bed in the rectory at wind-swept Notre Dung hoping—when he knew there was no hope—that his mother's dreams might come true. That one day he would stand tall and true in New York City's famous Rainbow Room and preach of end-time events to the most influential people in the world. Every wild-eyed evangelist on the planet went after the poor, the masses, the downtrodden. Clifford had a different ministry. He would be a minister to media moguls, literary agents, actors, music industry executives. Every evangelist knows that the poor have souls, but they are inclined to forget that TV personalities have them too. The talk show hosts, the child stars, the shining, chatty, dazzling types who host New Year's Day Parades. Clifford Clemp would harvest those souls for Jesus.

Now he knew that the dream was more than a pepperoni-induced wish. It was real. He would no longer be Clifford Clemp, nut case proprietor of a wacky roadside attraction. He would be a warrior for the Lord. No longer a foot soldier in the Christian army, but a general. A maverick general in a silver jacket.

When he looked up, DeBack and Concho were watching him, uncertain of his next move. Concho stood on his toes, tense and bewildered at the unprecipitated outburst of tears. DeBack eyed Clemp with an air of watchfulness.

Clemp held up the jacket.

"It's just like my mother's dream," he said, beaming through tear-soaked eyes. "She sees me wearing a silver jacket—this silver jacket—preaching to the important people in New York City's famous Rainbow Room."

"Oh," Concho said, as if all was explained.

DeBack held back, looking unconvinced.

Clemp shook the jacket at DeBack. "This is the sign, the sign I've been waiting for. The sign that I have a work to do."

"Well, I hate to burst your bubble," DeBack said slowly, making a salesman-like sucking sound in his back molars. "But it's not exactly your jacket. It's mine."

A long pause followed as Clemp fought through a jungle of emotion, fighting to speak the words that weighed on his heart.

"I haven't got much in the way the world counts riches," he began, "But I'd give all that."

"You got that plane," DeBack comforted.

"I." Clemp's mouth popped shut. His gaze shot over to the plane. "Well, uh..." he groped for words.

"Buuuut," DeBack said, "If you don't think it's worth it." DeBack reached out for the jacket.

"If we took the plane you could always flag down the Greyhound from El Paso," Concho said helpfully.

Clemp nodded, clutching the jacket. His eyes filled with tears. "You're right. Take it. Take the plane. Where I'm going I ain't got no use for it."

"Deal?" DeBack asked, holding an outstretched hand.

Clemp nodded again, dumb with tearful joy. "Deal," he whispered hoarsely and the two shook on it.

♌♌♌

The wooden body of the plane rattled and shook. Clouds slipped by like marshmallows resting on a blue tablecloth.

"So how does a snake know how to fly a plane?" Concho shouted from the back seat.

"To survive, you adapt," DeBack replied from the pilot's cockpit, surveying the world below through Clifford Clemp's smudgy goggles.

The small plane buzzed over the landscape, which was beginning to turn from Texas burnt brown to a shade of yellow, now streaked with hints of green. And undulating gently with small hills, trees and lazy winding streams.

"You're dancing around the question," Concho shouted, wincing in the wind. Lack of goggles preventing his seeing DeBack.

"We snakes had wings in the garden, you know."

Here he was at it again, Concho thought. The garden this, the garden that. Just like some people were about their high school football team. Their glory days.

"So you had wings," Concho shouted. "Still doesn't mean you know how to fly a plane."

A long silence from up front.

"Listen," DeBack said. "I could still bite you. Even in this form."

Concho shook his head. "Jeez. I'm just making conversation."

Concho settled back in the seat. The ripping of the wind, the drone of the engines, and his own acute hunger made him tired, zapped of energy. When would he eat again? The plane had passed over a handful of small towns, but DeBack ignored his pleas to land for a quick bite. At one point the plane flew so low over a Taco Bell Concho smelled the tacos and chicken burrito supremes. Tears sprang to his eyes.

His head lolled against the back of the seat. He'd been so panicked about the end of the world, he'd only slept in snatches the night before. Now that he had seen what was coming—even though he had no idea what it was—his blood pressure had dropped a little. Seeing your enemy was better than not seeing it. At least you could plan a little.

And besides, DeBack had said the two of them would ride it out together.

The two of them.

What a strange partnership, Concho thought. Here he was a complete amnesiac who didn't even know where his clothes had come from, flying across Texas with a snake in human form.

And not just any snake, but *The Snake*. The snake of snakes. A true celebrity. The old serpent in the garden. The old serpent who'd tricked a stupid, gullible Eve. Not to mention stupid, gullible Clifford Clemp. An airplane for a jacket? Holy Mother Tabasco.

Stupid...gullible...

He would have to watch his back. And his front. And above all—he'd have to watch what he ate.

Certainly no apples. Apples were out no matter how hungry he got. Apples had been the big mistake the first time around for poor Adam and Eve. His stomach gave a loud, spiraling gurgle. But he'd eat nothing from DeBack.

Concho closed his eyes and was swallowed up in the droning of the plane's engines, dozing off dreaming of food, lots of food.

Concho awoke in total darkness. Darkness mixed with wetness. And with a sickening, riding-up sensation in his stomach. He opened his eyes and listened for the plane's engine. Nothing. He decided that he was having hunger hallucinations. All the blood in his body seemed to be stampeding into his head. Concho reached forward, intending to tap DeBack on the shoulder, however, he found a strange resistance. Extending his arm turned into a quite a chore. A pressure crushed against him as though he were arm wrestling with an unseen force.

The wetness was increasing. A hard, pelting sensation. An increasing pressure in the pit of his stomach. And a pulling-back sensation on his face.

"DeBack!" Concho shouted.

"Yes?"

"What's happening? I have the feeling that something's not right."

"Really?" DeBack replied.

"Yes."

"Is this a psychic sense?"

"No," Concho said. "Not psychic."

"More physical?"

"Yes, more physical, I'd say. In my stomach. And my face seems to be fluttering. I think maybe I'm hallucinating."

"Ah."

"Is anything the matter?"

DeBack turned his head slightly, so Concho had a one-quarter view of his placid face. "We're just out of fuel."

A flash of lightning momentarily illuminated the storm cloud that the plane had spent the last several moments plunging through. Nose first.

Whipping rain stung Concho's face and he put up a hand to shield his eyes. The old wood and canvas plane shuddered badly. Small wires that held the tail and the wings to the body began popping off like guitar strings, twanging and flailing wildly. One whipped across his face. He waved his arms, fending them off. His insides pressed themselves against the bottom of his throat.

"Do something!" he shouted, reaching out to grip DeBack's shoulders. "Do something, you stupid reptile!"

Up front Concho could hear the sounds of the engine grinding. Occasional puffs of white smoke whipped past him.

"We're empty!" DeBack shouted.

"Do something!"

The plane fell out of the bottom of the cloud and through the broken struts and wings, Concho could see lights somewhere below.

The plane began a slow spin, the wings turning like the arms of a large grandfather clock, so that for a while the lights appeared to be in the sky and the rain seemed to shoot upward from the ground.

He could hear a long, terrified wail. Himself. Screaming.

DeBack managed to roll the plane back around as the lights got closer and closer, racing toward them like an explosion.

Then there was a roof with red tiles. One moment the roof was the size of a postage stamp. The next it filled the entire foreground like a drive-in movie screen.

Crash. Splinters of wood and red Italian tiles flew all about. Concho's body rammed against the back of his seat, his feet pressed hard on the floorboard as the roof rocketed past them in all directions.

In the top-story room of an apartment house, three people sprawled on a bed. A man, naked, tied to the four posters of a king size bed was being slathered in what looked like honey dijon dressing by two women in plastic wrap. The plane plowed through a lower floor—another savage jolt with pillars and posts flying all around—a woman was lying in a bath tub drinking a diet Pepsi as goldfish swam around her thighs. Another smashing, tearing. They found teenagers in the next room down smoking crack, listening to Tony Bennett. Another floor presented itself and was summarily smashed through. On the ground floor an Old English Sheepdog was committing an unnatural act with a plaid-colored footstool.

For a moment Concho closed his eyes, and stared at rings and spots floating in his mind. He waited for the long tunnel with the white light at the end. He waited for the floating-out-of-body sensation. But the only thing he ended up feeling was a spreading warm spot in the crotch of his pants.

He opened his eyes and gazed at the wreckage. When his mind could wrap itself around the situation, he realized that the biplane was dangling, swaying from the ceiling over a very surprised dog that had fled from the ottoman.

"DeBack," he said softly.

In reply, Concho heard a muffled voice. "Bgoftrks."

"Huh, what?"

"Bgoftrks."

The dog paced back and forth beneath the plane, swaying like a shabby chandelier. A low growl came from the animal's throat.

"What of tricks?" Concho asked.

"Bg!" Came the insistent answer in the kind of voice that comes from under several thick blankets.

"Bag of tricks?" Concho said. "Oh, the leather bag. With the apples, eyelash, cinnamon flavored gum, etc."

"Ys."

He began to search about the space where he was sitting. Only things on the floor were Clifford's empty bottles of Old Tennessee.

"Where's it at?"

"Upher."

"Where?"

"Upher."

"Up there?"

"Ys!"

"Up there with you?"

What followed was a string of incomprehensible swearing.

The huge dog now jumped at the plane, nudging it, pawing at it, increasing the pendular movement. Concho watched, sickened, as the floor swung back and forth faster and faster. The dog yipped and whined, jumping and nipping at this threatening, almost wingless object swaying above him.

A beam in the ceiling burped and groaned under the stress.

More muffled cursing and shrillness from up front.

"Good boy, good lassie," Concho murmured. "You don't want to do that, no you don't, no, no, no, no," he chided gently.

The sheep dog sat back on its haunches, barking, its tail-less back end wiggling.

The beam overhead groaned and squawked, then broke. The plane released, dropped another four feet, and landed on the ottoman.

The wreckage rested nose first for a moment, then crashed to the left, and turned upright. It destroyed the sofa, coffee table, TV and ripped down the mauve drapery.

When the hulk came to rest, Concho waited again, waited for a shattering of pain, a fountain of blood, an ache of some sort. Nothing. He felt okay. Slowly he crawled over the passenger's seat to the front cockpit. The light was not good. Rain poured through the newly ripped hole in the roof of the apartment house. He looked up the hole into the storm clouds rippling with lightning.

He peered into the cockpit, trying to find DeBack in a bundle of clothes and arms and legs.

Then he stopped and pulled away.

"DeBack?" his voice quivering. "Hey, hey, what the hell?"

The thing that had been DeBack's head now had arms sticking out the top. His nose and eyes were missing. A foot, with wiggling toes, was rearranged on his throat. A finger protruded out his shoulder.

"DeBack. You alive? Hey," Concho whispered through hands that had rushed to his mouth.

"Ys," replied the muffled voice. Imoky. Jstgetthbgotrks."

"Right. The bag of tricks," Concho said, rummaging through the tangle of body parts. "You're not bleeding," he said encouragingly.

"Hrryup."

"Okay, okay," Concho replied. He ripped open DeBack shirt and discovered two eyeballs in his chest staring out at him.

"Oh, my God," Concho burst out, covering his mouth, feeling a boulder of yuck lodged in his throat.

"Ovrther," said the voice. The eyeballs jerked several times toward the place where DeBack's feet would have been. "Ovrther!"

Concho gulped several times trying to ignore the taste of stomach acid. He stared into the darkness past the control stick. "Okay...I think I see it," he was able to say. His hand reached deeper and deeper into the cockpit until his fingers came to rest on the smooth leather bag. "Got it," he said pulling free.

"Apl," DeBack said.

"Apple?"

"Ys."

Concho reached inside and rummaged through the objects. He pulled out one of the pruny apples he'd picked for DeBack the day before.

"There's only two in here. Here we are," he said, holding up one of the wrinkled fruit in front of the eyeballs.

"Whrsothrwun?"

"Don't know. One must have fallen out during the crash. Only one left after this one."

"OK, ptieginmymuth."

"Do what?"

"Pt."

"Put?"

"Ieg."

"It?"

"Ys."

"Put it," Concho said.

"Inmymuth."

Concho concentrated for a moment, wiping the rain from his forehead. "Put it...in your mouth?"

"Brvo."

"Put it in your mouth."

Concho began to survey the rearranged thing that DeBack had become. He resembled one of those weird Picasso paintings.

"Um," Concho said. Picking up pieces of cloth and checking underneath. "Where is it?"

"Hurryup!"

"I can't find it!" Concho cried.

DeBack sighed, a long, drawn-out, gathering-patience sigh. "Marco," he said at last.

"Polo." Concho grinned.

"Marco."

"Polo." Concho turned the collections of parts over.

"Marco," the voice said clearly.

"Polo...hey..."

"Marco."

"Oh hey! Oh man!" Quivering, Concho drew back in bewilderment and disgust.

"What."

"I'm not putting it in therrrre!" Concho looked with alarm at the new site of DeBack's mouth. On the wrong side of his body, a little more than half way down. Lodged between muscular, brown butt cheeks.

"Just stick it in." DeBack demanded.

"I..."

"Hurry up!"

Concho's shoulders rode up. Okay. He swallowed once against the rising bile, closed his eyes and inserted the pruny apple into DeBack's new Chaucerian mouth opening.

With his eyes averted, Conch heard a series of grunts and then a long aaahhh of satisfaction. When he turned back around DeBack had recovered his shape. He checked to be sure that all of DeBack's pieces were back in proper alignment.

"Well?" DeBack demanded, holding up his shirt. "Well?" holding up both arms and turning around.

"Yeah..." Concho said. Eyeing him critically. "Yeah, I guess you're okay."

"Good," DeBack said, straightening his clothes, climbing out of the plane, into the living room.

"What the hell happened?"

The dog cocked its shaggy head, watching the two men deplane.

"Shape-shifting isn't a flawless thing, I mean, I'm still technically a snake," DeBack said, picking his way through the shards of broken furniture. "Take a hit like that and everything slides out of place."

Concho hopped out of the plane.

"You've done this before?"

"Mmm-hmm." DeBack nodded.

"When?"

DeBack held out his hand and Concho handed over the leather bag of tricks.

"Various times."

DeBack opened the front door of the house a crack and peered through rain falling out of the sky. Among the sheets of rain, half a dozen tall, glistening figures were approaching the apartment building. Flash lights bounced like dancing balls in the darkness.

"What's out there?" Concho asked.

Deback frowned and shook his head. "Looks like neighbors. Or the police. Bunch of guys with flashlights."

"What do we do?" Concho asked. "I think we mighta killed some people when we was coming through the roof. Maybe the guy tied to his bed."

DeBack strained to look through the crack in the door. "Sympathy," he mumbled.

"What? What'zat?"

"Act hurt. Get back in the plane."

"Huh? Wait, I..."

Something struck Concho across the mouth, hard. His head snapped back and as he fell forward, his forehead hit the door. He slid to the floor. Next thing he knew, DeBack was picking him up off the floor, dragging him back into the biplane.

"Yuh hit me." Concho said.

"Needed to be bleeding," DeBack whispered, sounding strangely pleased, arranging Concho in a twisted position.

"I'm bleeding?" he asked, gingerly touching the sides of his mouth.

"Moan."

Concho stared up at him. Spooked.

"Moan!" DeBack demanded. A dim red glow filling his eyes.

"Augh."

"No, softer."

"Augh."

"Again, with feeling."

"Auugh..."

"Perfect."

DeBack dropped the leather bag onto the cockpit floorboard. "One apple left in bag," he mumbled, foraging around beneath the seat.

"What're you doing?"

"Got to find that lost apple. Ah, I see it," his arm extended under the seat up to his shoulder. Grappling until the very tip of his fingers dug into the pruny apple, pulling it forward. He climbed down, stepped over to a corner of the room and tossed it down his throat. He crumpled like a balloon. After he had returned to snake form he slithered quickly toward the kitchen.

Concho missed the second half of the transformation—except for seeing a snake slithering toward the kitchen—when blood trickled into his eyes.

Seconds later, a scuffle of footsteps rumbled through the door. Concho was aware of heavy shoes and mumbling, and the room was full of flashlights. He watched as the figures picked their way through the rubble.

A brilliant light shown directly into his eyes.

"Over here, guys," a deep voice said. The other lights moved toward the plane. Arms reached up and pulled at what was left of the upper right wing, tossing it against the wall.

Concho squinted to get a look at the group.

A man with neatly clipped blond hair, wearing a green denim shirt and pleated chinos, bent over the plane, gazing at him thoughtfully.

"Are we under arrest?" Concho blurted.

The man, with a boyish middle-age face, smiled. "Welcome to Awareness, Missouri. My name is Turner. I'm not a police officer, I'm a caring nurturer."

"A what?"

"A caring nurturer, trained in skills such as low-impact persuasion," Turner smiled again, a warm skillful smile.

Turner and others reached down and began to lift Concho out of the plane.

"DeBack!" he called. "DeBack!"

"You hurt your spine?" one of the men asked.

"No, DeBack was the pilot.'

"Where is he?"

"I think he crawled into the kitchen," Concho said just before cracking his head on what was left of the overhead left wing.

"Hey! Oh, my God!" a voice shouted.

"A snake!" another voice shouted.

"A rattler!"

"De-Back!" Concho hollered. "De-Baaaaaak!"

Concho pressed his head to his knees, hunched in the back of the bouncing transportation vehicle. Outside, torrential rain buffeted the truck and water leaked through the green canvas covering. The roar of the storm mixed with the heavy grinding of gears.

At intervals, Concho raised up his wet head and stared at the guard seated opposite him. The burly man with a whisk-broom mustache wore a black t-shirt that read, *Practice Random Acts of Kindness*.

This was the end of the trail as far as Concho was concerned. In his mind, he began to sense that this was an extended imminent-death experience, like in that story, *The Incident at Owl Creek* where a guy is just about to swing from the gallows and in a split second before his death, his mind created an extended and vividly real escape scenario.

The jungle dream. Texas wasteland. The snake. The cave glyphs. Now this—Awareness, Missouri.

A sense of chilly fate hedged in around him. Whatever was happening, it was all out of his control. As if he were tied to the back of a Peterbilt with Lucifer at the wheel. There was nothing left but to ride it out.

His eyes were on the guard again.

"Takin' me to jail?" Concho asked in puny voice.

The guard shook his head. "No."

Concho's hesitated, his face skewering up. Surprised. Jail seemed like the next logical step.

"Where you takin' me then?" he asked after a bit.

"The Dialogue Center." The guard's voice was casual, even friendly.

Concho shivered in his wet clothing. "Dialogue...um...what's that?"

"You'll spend some time there dialoguing with the coordinator."

"Dialoguing. Oh. You mean, just talk to someone for awhile?"

The guard nodded with a neighborly smile that seemed to say, now you've got it.

Concho sat up a little more, glancing around the back of the truck. Maybe things weren't so bad. If he was just gonna talk.

"What's your name? Oh, never mind," he huffed in embarrassment, nodding to a name tag pinned on the man's shirt. "Dan?"

"Dan," the guard nodded.

"Mine's Concho."

"Where you from, Concho?"

"Wisconsin, Dan."

"Really, what part?"

Concho hesitated. "All over," he laughed. "Just here and there, I guess."

"I was up in Wisconsin once," Dan said.

"Oh yeah? Fishing? Hunting?"

"No," Dan responded, fingering the barrel of his large flashlight. "Went up for a men's estro-gent weekend."

"A what kind of?"

"Estro-gent weekend. For men."

"Oh, I see." He didn't.

"It was very cleansing."

"Mmm-hmm. Must've been, must've been," nodding.

Dan got a faraway look for a second, then snapped back. "We Guys are so into our testosterone," he said, gesturing with hammy hands and thick forearms. "Everything is testosterone. You forget sometimes that you've got estrogen in your veins too. You just forget." he chuckled. "Lucky for us we got Sister Gaia to help remind us."

"Yeah..." Concho said, and lapsed back into silence, trying to avoid making eye contact with the guard. "Estrogen? Sister GeeGaw?"

"Gaia," Dan corrected. "She's our spiritual and political leader."

A moment later the truck bumped to a stop. The back of the truck opened and in a dim light Concho could make out glistening forms of several men in yellow rain ponchos. The parking lot looked like a rising river, with streamers of dark mud snaking through the fast-rushing currents.

Concho hopped out and was led into an attractive office building with the words, *Dialogue Center*, etched frostily into the glass of the sliding front doors.

Surrounded by the small knot of men—all of whom bore relaxed, confident expressions on their faces—Concho moved through a lobby full of slender green plants and body-contoured chairs in black, seamless Italian leather. Then down a long beige hallway dotted with neat bulletin boards and signs that offered on-the-job safety tips and diagrams of emergency exits. Gently, he was led into a spacious room furnished with several over-stuffed couches and a dozen large recliners. At the far end of the room stood two ping-pong tables, more plants, and posters of European port cities. The walls held a number of sizable paintings depicting vague swaths of color, all very subdued, pleasant, non-threatening works designed to put-at-ease those who know nothing about art.

Concho sat at one end of a bulky couch. He sunk in as if lowered onto a giant marshmallow cloud. He let out a sigh. The biplane had shaken him to the core all day, the seat had been an uncushioned board. The transport truck had been steely and uncomfortable. Now this pillowed ecstasy. He felt weak and shaky with pleasure.

He looked around the room, undertoned but cushy. He took in the circle of men dropping themselves into various comfortable poses on the surrounding furniture. They wore open-necked shirts and Timberline walking shoes. The words *group therapy* came to him.

He closed his eyes, lolled his head back and listened as the search party folded and set aside their rain ponchos, speaking in quiet voices.

Concho felt a presence standing over him and opened his eyes.

A tall, lean man with pronounced shoulders, a thrusting chin and a lank of dark hair falling down one side of his middle-aged face peered down at him.

Concho lifted one hand, holding it out, "Name's Concho."

"Hello," the other replied, shaking hands, "I'm Rick. I'm the coordinator.

Rick wore no uniform, no badge. With his pony tail, silvered with streaks of gray, he looked like a graphic designer or a junior college philosophy instructor.

"Coordinator Rick," Concho murmured. "Didn't you use to be a Ranger?"

Rick stared at Concho, winced out a shallow smile.

"We're just gonna...dialogue, right?" Concho tried to maintain a calm, congenial demeanor. But his palms were sweaty.

"That's right." An affable smile came to Rick's face, a wide mouth with teeth like white Chiclets. "We'll just do a little positive befriending."

For some reason, Concho thought he said the last word as one might say, "beheading." "Friending?"

"Let you vocalize a little. Put your remembering skills to work."

"Uh-huh," Concho said sleepily.

Rick sat beside Concho and put both of his long arms on the back of the couch.

"I understand we had some unpleasantness tonight," again smiling. Then the smile faded and Rick's face took on the aspect of a counselor at a summer camp who is concerned about an outbreak of poison oak. "Some community persons have been badly injured."

"Uh," raised one voice on the far couch, "killed, actually."

"Killed, then," Rick said. "Started the Great Journey. Networking with the other side."

"We didn't mean no harm." Concho began.

"And an apartment house destroyed," Rick continued, going doe-eyed with disappointment. "Lives disrupted, the well-being of our community overturned. All of us at home interacting with our loved ones. Forced out into this nasty weather really interrupts the bonding process."

"I'm sorry," Concho mumbled. He glanced in uneasy fashion from side to side. "Really, I am."

"I was parenting," said one voice.

"I was helping my son with his kitchen learning skills," rumbled a second voice. "Spoiled a perfectly good souffle."

"At my wife's birthing class," said a third.

"On such a night..." Rick said, clearly dismayed. He thought for a second, or at least, gave the impression of thinking, then said, "Perhaps, Concho, you could focus on what happened. Just scroll back a little and share, if you would, the events that led up to this evening's problem."

Concho shifted and made several humming noises. "I don't recollect much. Exactly. I was in the plane. Then we was crashing through the apartment house. And there was a dog humping a footstool."

Rick nodded a number of times. "Okay. Okay. Excellent. We've gotten off to a good start."

This remark was followed by a general chorus of affirming, mmm-hmm's.

"Now," Rick said, "let's rewind again. And perhaps, Concho, you could dilate your mind a little. And share a few more of the details. We need some factualizing."

"I don't remember nothing more."

"Concho, please, just relax, let your thoughts go."

"There ain't nothin' else."

"But if you could transition back."

"There ain't nothin' more to tell. You moron." Concho's eyelids jiggled. "I was in the back seat."

"Concho!" Rick's voice boomed. A scarlet spot appeared in the center of his forehead. His earlobes glowed red.

Concho's eyes bugged.

"I think it's only fair to tell you," Rick said, his voice lowering, "that I am a victim of Sudden Anger Syndrome."

Concho relaxed a little and gazed at Rick, with no expression, no idea how to react to that statement. The people in this town talked another language. Most words ending in *ing*. What were they talking about? And Sudden Anger Syndrome, didn't that used to be called hot headed?

Rick continued, "I've gone into a Twelve-step program, Angerholics Anonymous. Al over there is my anger-mentor."

A thin, agreeable fellow across the room nodded. A name tag on his chest read Al.

Concho nodded, then looked around the room. The other men's heads nodded in sympathetic understanding. Hey-man-we've-been-there-too, nods. No doubt they also suffered, each of them, from syndromes that hungered for a solution in twelve steps.

"What?" Concho groped for words. "Where am I?"

Rick gave him a crooked smile. "You've landed in Awareness, Missouri. We're a model community. An experiment, if you will, in the futuring of humanity. We're all caring nurturers—of each other, of the land, of our community." Pronouncing it, cuh-mu-ni-ty, adding an extra syllable somewhere. "Under the leadership of Sister Gaia."

"Who is this Sister Gaia?" Concho winked and nudged his elbow in Rick's direction. "Is she like Mother Teresa, or something? Like, the nun that runs things around here?"

"Too much Testosterone." Rick shook his head sadly. The others joined him. "Makes you lose all respect."

Concho stared up at the ceiling, thinking, "if I close my eyes, they will go away."

ᔕᔕᔕ

In 1677, a trapper, the oldest son of a French furniture maker named Coulou, traveled to the Missouri river, attempting to escape the outrage of an entire tribe of Cherokees. While the warriors of this tribe had been away on a spiritual quest involving long weeks of travel and late-night herbal smokes, Junior Coulou had single-handedly impregnated every village woman of child-bearing potential who'd been left behind.

He traveled by night. One midnight, weeks later, he lay pitched forward in the mud, panting on a knoll by the river. Prongs of lightning split the night firmament. Treetops thrashed against the dark, descending sky. A summer storm erupted and the pummeling rain was washing away all traces of his escape. His scent, his tracks, the trail of broken leaves, branches, scuffed rocks.

Reveling in the success of his run for freedom, Coulou rose and lifted his arms to heaven. Rain spattered his wild bearded face. He was cold, tired, hungry and he was thousands of miles from France.

Thankful, he took a moment, with face upturned, to shout praises to Jehovah for sparing his life.

There on the knoll, he fashioned a crude cross from pieces of wood, lashed together with a leather thong. He pounded the cross into the ground and consecrated that land to the betterment of mankind.

Coulou lived on the site for several months giving shouts of hosanna to the Almighty until, insane with syphilis, he tried to eat a live Copperhead snake.

Coulou's story did not die with him.

The wooden cross was a testament of his love for womankind. But the cross eventually fell over. Rotted.

Vultures nipped away at Coulou's body. Foxes carted off his bones and ants did the rest.

However, Coulou's spirit lived on, hazing around in the after life for an inordinate period of time. Several hundred years. Until he was accidentally reincarnated when a bolt of lightning hit a kennel during a particular sensitive meeting between two old English Sheep dogs. The pick of the litter was named Bobby. A sexual dynamo with a heady lust for household furniture. And as karma would have it, he lived within spitting distance of the place where Coulou died, the knoll by the Missouri river.

A place he had dedicated in God's name to the betterment of future generations.

A place now called Awareness.

♌♌♌

"Our community," Rick continued, "was originally a very spiritual place. Local Indian lore has it that a god died here. Much as, I imagine, our own dying-god myth in Western thinking. Maybe you've read my book, "*Merchandising Myth?*"

Concho shook his head.

"No...well," Rick went on, "In it, I talk about—actually, I talk about a lot of things—but I *do* make mention that there is even a cross symbology tied to this place. A very healing, very spiritual place. Sometimes, if you walk along the river early in the morning you can feel harmonic vibrations, the spiritual centeredness of this place."

Rick stood. "I like to think that this is still a spiritual place. That we are the guardians of that rich heritage. In fact," he directed Concho's gaze to a framed sign over the door, "that's our motto over there."

The sign read: *Awareness, Missouri—A Tradition of Heritage.*

"I like to think that we walk the same ground as the god who died here and of the shamans who followed after him."

Concho watched as Rick ambled toward an orange door at the far end of the room, just past the ping-pong tables.

"Al, Dan," the coordinator said, "bring him into the Healing Room. The rest of you can go."

Concho felt himself being hoisted up by the arms. Al and Dan smiled down at him with supportive, friendly smiles.

The others in the room rose, relieved at being released from their duties. They could now return to their homes to continue their dutying there.

Good men, Concho thought, solid men with wives and families, who took parenting seriously and who held to community standards.

As he was being lugged across the room, Concho felt ashamed that he had intruded on this town. Had destroyed property and interrupted cheerful and significant evenings at home.

"What's the Healing Room?" Concho asked.

"You'll talk to the counselor," Dan replied, grunting a little at the strain.

"I could walk," Concho offered.

"No, thanks," Al said. "It's better if we drag you."

"Oh?"

"Helps improve the psycho-drama."

"Ah..."

When they reached the orange door, the two large men kicked the door open and flung Concho into the room. He hit shoulder first, rolled and ended up on his back. Al and Dan then yanked him to his feet, nearly dislocating his shoulders.

Concho was on his feet again only for a moment. One of the men punched him in the gut while the other shoved him into a large, comfortable easy chair. He looked around without really seeing anything. His stomach hurt and his breath wheezed. When he realized he wasn't in for any more punching or yanking, he settled into the chair and cautiously took in his surroundings.

The small room was lit entirely by fat, opium-scented candles and the walls were lined with books in slim glass book shelves. Across from Concho sat a man with a glassy stare wearing thick-rimmed glasses and a black goatee. Concho stared at the man until he realized where he'd seen him before.

Concho turned to Dan, standing guard at the left side of the chair.

"It's Rick," Concho said.

"Shhhh," Dan responded.

Concho turned to Al, guarding the right side.

"But it's Rick with a false beard and glasses," Concho insisted.

Without looking, Al's side-of-beef hand reached out and thwacked Concho on the side of the head.

"Hey," Concho mumbled, rubbing his head. "Come on."

"Good evening," the counselor said. When he spoke, the candle light reflected off the clear plastic tape backing on the goatee.

Concho sighed. "Good evening Rick," he said, in a bored voice.

"My name is Dr. Gruber. How are you feeling tonight?"

"I'm fine, Rick."

Dr. Gruber lifted his hand, vaguely indicating the right side of Concho's head. Al whomped Concho again.

"Ow, damn."

"My name is Dr. Gruber," said the counselor. "How are you feeling tonight?"

"Fine. That is until you guys started whacking around on my head," he said, nursing his jaw. "Fine, Dr. Gruber. Just fine."

"Tonight, we must assess your mental stability," the counselor said. "I will ask some questions and you will answer."

Concho sighed and ran his tongue around his molars. The world was ending. He and DeBack needed to be heading out.

"Listen," Concho said. "If you'd please just let me go....I'm sorry the plane plowed through that apartment house. I'm sorry you all had to come out tonight. If there's anyway I could turn back the hands of time...."

The counselor lifted both hands and both men blammed Concho, one on each side of his head.

"Augh...dang." Concho doubled over, his face screwed up. "Augh," he moaned, holding his head.

One of the men grabbed a handful of hair and yanked him back to an upright sitting posture.

"Hey! This ain't fair!"

The counselor gave Concho a my-soul-has-been-surgically-removed stare. The whites of his eyes were large, his pupils shrunken to dots.

"Tonight, we must assess your mental stability," said the counselor in a voice like dripping ice water. "I will ask some questions and you will answer them."

"And what if I don't?"

"If we should discover some instability..." the counselor said, a shrug in his voice. "You may require certain types of—shall we say—therapy?"

The counselor smirked and emitted a gassy, self-congratulatory ripple of laughter.

"What's therapy?" Concho asked, going into a cold panic. "What's therapy? Come on, hey..."

Concho heard a snicker. A brilliant light shone in his eyes.

The voice of the counselor soothed from across the room, "You are so tired, Concho. Tired and sleepy. You want to let your head roll back...so tired. Just listen to the sound of my voice..."

The room faded away and was replaced by a pink cotton candy spin. He waved his arms, fighting to connect through the sticky morass with memories he couldn't quite reach.

Then he was sitting with a woman in a bed of cool, soft leaves and pink rose petals. Strands of hair clung to her teary face. Her thin nostrils were red and her eyes were buried in her hands.

"I'm so cellulitey," she said softly.

"You're not," Concho whispered, drawing her nearer.

She had dark hair, olive skin. A pile of ringlets pitched forward, hair covered her face.

"It's so horrible, so ugly." She rubbed her eyes with her open hands.

"What's come over you?" he said.

"I'm nothing but cellulite," she whimpered, looking up with tear-stained deep brown eyes.

"I've never seen it," he said, stroking the side of her face. "Never."

She searched his face, a sad, surprised, wanting look.

"You've just never seen it. But you've felt it...every time...."

"No, no. I've never felt anything." His eyes reflected the light filtering through the boughs and branches overhead.

"It's the cellulite you can't see or feel that's the worst," she said. "It's the worst kind," she repeated.

"What's happened? Please tell me."

Panic filled her eyes. "Nothing. Nothing at all."

♌♌♌

With the ottoman buried underneath the wreckage of the biplane, the Old English Sheep dog blundered upstairs where small groups of men with flashlights were taking notes and snapping photographs. The crack-smoking teenagers were sprawled out dead on the second floor while other men dutifully cleaned up.

The dog nosed about the area, then flumped up the next flight of stairs where a woman in a bathtub was being lifted out of the water and into a large gray-green plastic bag. Goldfish were being flushed down the toilet. The dog backed away from a large hole in the roof that allowed in buckets of rain.

After the final run of stairs the dog sat and watched as a man on the large bed was being photographed. Two women in shiny Saran Wrap—shaken, but alive—were being questioned.

"We'll need to take you to the Dialogue Center," a man was saying.

"No, please," one of the women sobbed. "Please."

"We didn't mean any harm," begged the other woman.

The man shook his head. His face was lit weirdly by the flashlight he held. "Community standards," he said, writing notes on a note pad. "You know what Sister Gaia says about Pornography."

As the dog padded from room to room, some ancient, ghostly parts of its brain sensed that things were not as they should be. Things were out of whack. There had never been a large, biplane-sized hole running vertically through the building before. None of the people in the house had ever been dead before.

And the men with the flashlights were a new, unwelcomed addition.

The dog took the steps carefully going back down, stiff-legging them with his front legs and bouncing a lot on his haunches. He wandered into the kitchen, lapped water from his round metal dish and stared at one of his favorite chairs. A wicker chair with an arousing colorful southwestern print pillow in the seat. But somehow, the desire for the chair had abandoned him.

His whole world had changed and he would need to sit and lick himself for awhile.

Then he saw it.

Red-hot canine adrenaline zapped his tiny brain.

A slithery something. Was it his imagination? No.

A growl rose in his throat and his tail-bobbed back end quivered with excitement.

There crawling along the base board was a large rattlesnake. A diamondback. It disappeared behind a hutch.

The Old English Sheep dog sniffed along the baseboard in the kitchen. He tried to push his basketball-sized head under the lip of the cabinets until his eyes were pulled back into slits. Sniff. Sniff.

Wait. A sound. A slither.

There.

Under the table. He leaped, scattering chairs in all directions, knocking the table on end. A cascade of plates and silverware clattered against the wall. He sniffed about the carnage, his head jerking from side to side. Ready to pounce, to kill, to maim. His large wet nose hoovered the air. His sniffing stopped. The large head lifted. Nothing. No snake.

He bounded into the living room, tongue lolling, ears flapping. He barked, sat for a moment searching the room, a mat of hair obscuring his vision. He stood.

There, again! A sound. A stifled rattle.

The dog made noises like an air compressor, a rapid snuff, snuff, snuff, snuff, plowing his face through the wreckage in the living room, following an unmistakable reptile scent. Listening for more give-away sounds of snake activity.

The dog clumsily, unsteadily, clambered atop the body of the airplane. He was close now. He shook all over in the attempt to stay upright on the veneered surface of the plane. Dog toenails left white scratch marks on the wood finish.

He dipped his head into the back seat but smelled nothing more than old liquor bottles. With a quick leap, he slid into the front seat. Here the game grew serious. A potent snake smell rose up out of this part of the plane.

The dog bobbed his head into the blackness of the cockpit and just as quickly pulled his head out. The scent was powerful. The danger of a snake hurtling out of the darkness made him extra wary. Again, he dipped his head into the cockpit. No attack. He dipped his head in again. Still no attack.

Emboldened, he dropped his two front paws into the seat and went about the business of sniffing in earnest. The snake had once again eluded him, but one object presented a powerful attraction.

A leather bag.

Mmm, leather. Good chewing.

The sheep dog gripped the bag in his teeth and backed out of the cockpit. He looked around and realized he couldn't jump with the bag in his teeth. Too cumbersome.

The dog dropped the bag on what was left of the body of the plane and jumped down. Once on the floor, he twisted around in circles and began to nip at the edge of the bag. It was farther from the floor than his canine math had calculated. He jumped at the bag, again gripping little fibers, loosening its hold.

He dropped back to pant. Let his tongue loll out. As he did, his head cocked to one side, noticing that the bag had begun to slide. At first, he could hardly detect any movement, then it went a little faster. The contents of the bag shifted inside. Something small and round dropped out of the bag and the sheep dog caught it in his teeth, chewed once and swallowed.

The things had a strange taste. Not like his dog food nor like the scraps of meat and leather he found in the woods. It had a mushy, sweet flavor. He licked his lips, not sure he approved of the taste it left in his mouth.

As the dog felt a hot glow in the pit of his stomach, he heard a noise from the plane. There, peering over the edge of the plane was the snake. Its eyes were large.

"My Apple. You ate my latht apple," the snake hissed.

DeBack watched, head swaying, tongue flicking with disgust as the Old English Sheep dog turned into a big naked, flabby man, covered with white hair. He looked remarkably like Kenny Rogers.

"Weird." The dog man looked down at himself, searching the acreage of his hairy belly. He bent lower, stopped, looking perplexed, bent lower still.

"Weird," the dog man said again, his voice deep, rattling, unnerved. He ran his woolly hands down his thick buttocks and the backs of his legs, feeling his new skin, new contour.

"You've turned into a man," DeBack said in an informative voice, lifting his triangular head to get a better look at this new creature. "Of courth you haven't really turned into a man. Jutht a thort of facthimile. Don't worry, it'll eventually wear off. It only latht ath long ath the apple ith in your body. When you path it you'll turn back into a dog. But for me it ith different. I eat one turn into a rattlethnake, eat another turn into a man."

"I don't care. I'm experiencing something. Something different. And right now it's my bottom. It kinda hurts," he complained. "So do my shoulders. And my head....damn, my head really hurts!"

The woolly hands clamped both sides of the large hairy head.

"It all wearth off," DeBack assured him. The fat, lengthy snake curled upon the biplane's body. "Nothing ith really permanent, you know."

"Hot damn! I don't care," the dog man trumpeted, leaping into the air, spinning circles, crashing around the room. A wide, white grin of triumph filling his face. "Yes! Yes! Yes!" he chanted, dancing a wild, arm-snapping mamba.

DeBack watched this display, his slits-for-eyes moving around quickly, trying to comprehend the meaning of this strange behavior.

"Oh, yeah! Oh yeah!" the dog man continued, overjoyed, awestruck, pirouetting around in the dark, in the shower of rain, his eyes downward, his hands now cupping some new possession.

"What? What ith it?" DeBack demanded.

The dog man whirled around. "A pecker!" he whooped, he yodeled. "I have a pecker! A pe-heh-heh-heh-heh-heh-cker!" he sang in spasmodic joy.

"Didn't you have one before?"

"Well yeah," the dog man reeled back. "A dog's pecker. But do you see any other dogs around? Huh? No. But there are lots of..." He grinned, wagging a finger. "...women. Hee, hee."

"Rarely a thortage of them," DeBack agreed.

"Do you know how sick I am of furniture? All the female dogs in this community have been fixed. 'Don't want any unwanted puppies now, do we?' Yesss." He bowed low to get a good look over the summit of his belly. "There it is," he murmured, as though peering into the frilly carriage of an apple-cheeked newborn. "A penis. My real, human, thunder-wonder, down-under plunder stick."

He reared up, gripping his new toy, thrust forward in both fists. "I wanna use it! I need to use it!" he panted. "See how it works."

The dog man fell to the floor, stretching out his full length, his whole unclothed body wriggling. A kind of uncontainable doggy rapture. He was full of elongated sighs, squirmy noises, woofing and growling.

"What's your name?" DeBack called out over this Hallelujah chorus.

The dog man ceased moving instantly. And he sat up attentively. "I'm Bobby. My name is Bobby."

"Bobby."

"Yes."

"I can get you all the womanhood you want."

"Yeah?" The eyes narrowed. "But I want a lot...a whole lot. Yes."

DeBack's head inched slowly forward. "I can get you more than you can thtand."

"Oh, I wouldn't stand. No. Not exactly," Bobby said, shifting onto his hands and knees. "It'd be more a position like..."

"No, no," DeBack interrupted. "I mean I can get you more than you can handle. I can get you tho much female firepower, it'll blow that thing you're packing right through your head."

Bobby's eyes went vacant. His imagination was a small universe whose outer edge had been reached. He stared at DeBack with something like creeping terror in his large eyes.

"Wow." Then he shook his head viciously. He looked up again, all eyes. "Wow."

Footsteps. Thudding, thick-soled Timberlands.

DeBack's eyes shot a glance to the staircase.

"Hide," he said.

"Where?"

"Inside. Jump inside the plane."

The footsteps grew louder, drawing closer.

"I can't fit in there," Bobby said, moving toward the plane, poking his head inside the front cockpit.

Four large brown shoes appeared one by one, slowly, deliberately from an upper stair.

"In the kitchen. Thchnell! Thchnell!" DeBack hissed.

Bobby backed up, tripped on a chair and more or less fell head-over-heels through the kitchen door, skating aftward on his furry behind.

Two men, mumbling, making small explaining gestures with their hands, made their way down the stairs. Reaching the base of the staircase, they stopped for a moment, consulting notebooks by flashlight, comparing each other's impressions of the carnage upstairs. They glanced up, hearing a slight, dry rattle. Two brilliant flashlight beams shone slowly across the room revealing an upturned sofa with stubby, upraised legs. A badly scratched piano.

Crooked paintings. A black, curtainless window densely spattered with rain.

The beams of light traveled down the body of the biplane, golden tracers appearing when the lights moved through the torrent of rain plummeting through the ceiling.

Nothing unusual after a plane crashing into an apartment house, they agreed. Their shoes sloshed across the soaked carpet and the two dark figures made their way toward the front door.

A moment later the living room appeared to be empty.

♌♌♌

The counselor, in a show of patience, removed his glasses and balanced them on his knee.

"Concho," he said, "I think you're being evasive. Now let me ask you again—why do you keep saying *we? 'We* crashed,' or '*We* were in the plane.'"

"It was me and the snake. You saw the snake." He looked to Al and then Dan for agreement.

They both nodded. They'd seen the snake at the scene of the crash.

"And who was flying the plane. Hmm?" The counselor squirmed joyfully. "The snake? Had his little rattler wrapped around the joy stick? Hmm?"

Concho gazed at his feet. What should he say?

"And where is this snake?" Dr. Gruber searched Concho's face and then turned to the two men at his side. The counselor shrugged.

"I don't know where," Concho mumbled. "He...I guess he's still at the house."

"Well, in this community, we take pet ownership very seriously," Gruber said. "We have very strict leash laws and the homeowners association has a long list of do's and don'ts when it comes to..."

"I'm just saying..." Concho began.

"Yes?"

"I'm just..."

"The doctor is in," he cooed, waiting for Concho to respond. When he got nothing, he went on to say, "Well, I think that when you say, *we,* you're simply talking about yourself," the counselor announced. "Not some reptile friend of yours."

Concho shook his head.

"So right now," the counselor went on, "I'm talking to Concho. But when you were hypnotized a few minutes ago I felt I was talking to someone else. Someone who was sitting in a pile of leaves with his girlfriend? His hunny bunny? Hmm?"

"That's not it, that's...no...not it."

The counselor leaned forward. "Who are you, Concho? Tell me about yourself. Tell me about your family, mom and dad. Tell me about the time when you were a baby and dad threw you too high or about the time mom looked both ways and then touched your little acorn when she thought no one was looking."

"I can't," Concho said, on the verge of tears. "I don't remember nothing."

"Don't remember mom and dad? Don't remember Wisconsin?" the counselor shrieked in melodramatic astonishment. He whipped the glasses back on. Time for business.

"How about where you work? What you do for fun? Your favorite color?"

Concho shook, his lips tightened together.

"How far back does your memory go?"

Concho was slumped forward now, wiping at his eyes. "I can't remember nothing up to yesterday, 'round noon time."

"What happened? Share, share, share..."

"I can't," Concho said, his voice breaking. He knew the counselor was really coordinator Rick in a false beard and prescriptionless glasses. But the urge to confess, to rid himself of his unmanageable confusion, had risen up in his chest like a bubble needing to burst. "I can't," he whimpered.

Al and Dan were now kneeling on either side of him, giving him supportive shoulder pats and offering little words of encouragement.

"We're here, man. Give it up, go on, give it up." Al rubbed his shoulders. "If Big Bro's got you man...?"

"Big Bro?"

"The government. Big Brother. The Establishment." Al quick-chopped Concho's shoulders lightly, expertly. "We can help. But you have to take the first step."

He could tell them, sure. But what would they do to him when he told them about a snake who turned into a man, about the future etched on a stone wall in a cave in Texas, about pruny apples. About the world's largest pile of rabbit poop, about a wordless, ancient, empty ache located somewhere south of his heart, but he didn't. Something wouldn't let the bubble pop. His mouth opened in soundless agony, ready to share his manly burden of pain, but the words didn't come to the surface. The only words his brain could pull together was about a World War I aircraft and they were flying toward the East Coast. His mouth hung open and finally a mid-range note emerged and hung in the air. No vibrato, no breaks for breath. A hard, throaty call. The sort that usually accompanies a wooden tongue depressor in a doctor's office.

Or an enema syringe.

For a time Al, Dan and Dr. Gruber hung on to that sound, recognizing it as the typical precursor to a confession. However, after several minutes, they began to grow restless. It was as if Concho's vocal chords had gotten stuck in the "on" position. Restlessness turned to impatience and then irritation. The counselor finally leaned back in his chair, crossed his legs and said, "Oh, for Christ sake, shut him up."

Al and Dan picked Concho up and tossed him against the far wall. On impact, his voice ceased. Concho stood up and brushed himself off, feeling, somehow cleansed. He had not needed to confess after all, he'd simply needed to let out a long *aaaaahhhhh* of unhappiness. A big mental purge.

He smiled.

"I'm really hungry," he said. "Could I have a burrito or something?"

The counselor sighed, flubbing his lips. "Concho, Concho, Concho."

"I'm famished," he said again, and reached to steady himself with the wall.

"And what about your therapy?" Gruber said.

"Doc, I just need some time to put it all together. I must've bumped my head on something when the plane crashed."

The counselor stared at Concho, light gleaming off the panes of glass in the glasses. "I've done all I can," he said. "You show a remarkable lack of cooperation, a complete lack of concern for the standards of our community, a very trenchant lack of understanding about the rights of the individual versus that large and more productive right of the community. The things that are important in our little corner of the world are things like parenting, friending, centering, facilitating, mentoring, dialoguing, nurturing. You appear to think only of Concho. Concho's needs. Concho's wants. You cling to outdated, eighteenth century ideas on the rights of the individual, the cant and dogma of the Jeffersons and the Paines. Pleasure must give way to responsibility."

The counselor stopped suddenly and waited for a response.

"I'd just really like a burrito," Concho said, collapsing on the floor, blacking out from lack of food.

He awakened some time later inside a 10 by 10 foot room with an unpainted cement floor, cement walls on three sides and a fourth that was made of metal bars. His head rested against a metal bunk with no mattress and his feet were propped against a white porcelain toilet with no lid.

When he asked where he was, Dan, the guard with the whisk-broom mustache replied, "We've secured a room for you here in The Caring Center."

"Looks like a jail to me," Concho said. His voice was weak and black spots were swirling around him like false beards and eyelashes. Through swimmy eyes he could make out the bars blocking his exit.

Dan smiled through his thatch of lip hair and a sparkle gleamed in his eyes.

"What?" Concho asked weakly. "What's so funny?"

Dan wiped at his eyes, a jolly red color had risen to his cheeks. "You're just so..." he shook his head, "...so twentieth century."

"What's that mean?"

"Well," Dan smiled, looking around, "I mean—jail?"

Concho sensed something was different about himself. He looked down and realized his clothing had changed. He now wore yellow pajama pants and a t-shirt that said, "Visualize World Peace."

"What happened to my clothes?" Concho asked.

"You soiled them when you passed out," Dan said.

"I dropped a load?"

Dan nodded.

"Thanks for getting me cleaned up. 'Preciate that."

Dan opened the metal door, "Let me know if there's anything you need."

"You sure this ain't jail?"

Dan shook his head, "This is not the Wild West," he said.

"So you bring me food?"

"Yes."

"You give me clothes to wear." Concho plucked at the yellow, flannel pants.

"Right."

"I sleep on this here cot."

Dan nodded. "We care for you. It's the Caring Center."

"And I can pretty much come and go as I please. Right?"

Lines in Dan's forehead deepened. "Where would you wanna go?"

"Just to get up and walk around, say. Get some fresh air."

Dan shook his head. "No, you can't just leave. We have to take care of you."

Concho nodded. "I get that." He gestured broadly. "But I'm just saying...if I *wanted* to, if I had it in my head that I *wanted* to kinda go outside, I could just open the door and go out. Right?"

Dan blinked. "Uh, I guess I don't understand. We take care of you here. This is the..."

"Caring Center," Concho said, beginning to feel a sense of heat on the back of his neck.

"Well..." Concern filling Dan eyes. "Don't get mad."

"Dan, this is jail. This is friggin' jail. You can call me old fashioned until the cows come home. But this is a friggin' jail!"

"This is a model community."

"This is a mind screw." Concho panted, pushing himself up on shaky arms and elbows.

Dan's eyes froze, his face wearing a sustained expression of fear.

"Al, hey, uh, Al," Dan called out.

Al showed up seconds later at the cell door. "What?"

"Say what you said. Just then. Just a minute ago," Dan said to Concho.

Concho hesitated. Now that he was calm again it sounded a little inappropriate. "I said ...this place is a ..."

"A..." Dan prompted.

"A...um," Concho looked away, "A mind screw."

Dan and Al exchanged glances. Al sighed and began rifling through papers on his clipboard.

"What?" Concho asked, his heart beginning to skip beats inside his chest. "What now?"

Al extended a pink sheet of paper. "Can you sign this, please?"

"What is it?"

"It's a waiver. It allows us to begin punching and kicking you again," he said.

"No thanks," Concho said indignantly, tossing the paper aside.

Dan opened the cell door and the two men began to punch and kick him anyway. Concho held up his hands to his face, trying to ward off their hammy fists and steel-toed designer boots. "Wait! I didn't sign nothin'! I didn't sign!" he shouted.

The two guards stopped pummeling him, stepped back and looked at Concho who was curled up on the cement floor.

"We'll continue to physically correct you until you sign the waiver," Dan said.

"Why?" Concho whimpered. "Why?"

"Pornographic language is against our community standards," Al replied. "Pornography of all kinds."

"Pornography by thought, pornography by word, pornography by deed," Dan chanted.

"Will you sign the waiver?"

"What if I don't?" Immediately Dan kicked him in the thigh and Al bent over and punched him in the face for what seemed like forever. "I'll sign! I'll sign," he finally groaned through bloodied lips.

"Great," Al said, handing the form down to him.

"Thanks."

With shaking fingers, Concho signed the form and handed it up to Al, who folded it neatly and placed it back on the clipboard.

"Thanks a mill," he said, leaving the cell.

Dan paused at the door. "Would you like a beverage?"

"Whisky," Concho breathed.

"Hmm, well...we're all alcohol-free here. Wanna Sharp's?"

Feeling like a punching bag, Concho shook his head and lay down on the cold floor. Sick and dizzy from a lack of anything to eat or drink. Battered, bruised.

"Mineral water?" Dan called out, clanging the door shut.

"Sure," Concho whispered.

"Wedge of lemon?"

Concho nodded. "Thanks."

Dan left and Concho called out after him, but the man was gone.

What did they want with him? The plane had crashed—by accident! They'd run out of fuel. They meant no harm.

Unless... No.

Concho shifted position, stood shakily and laid down on the cot. Was this something that DeBack had cooked up? Did these Awareness people know something he didn't?

Concho sighed. His body ached all over. His thoughts meandered aimlessly down the hallways of his mind. Could he be an unwitting participant of an evil plan? A serpent-related scheme? Some new horror of biblical proportion about to be unleashed?

He groaned and wondered if any of this was real.

Then she was there again. Dark skin, dark downcast eyes, long and perfect fingers covering her mouth. She gazed levelly at him, weeping softly, surrounded by soft, green boughs, an enchanted bed of fronds and rose petals.

"It's the little mountains of cellulite you can't see..."

She reached out for him, her apricot lips mouthing a name...his name, yet not his name. He felt a new misery, a muffled, buried pang of sorrow and loss, a hard, knotted, calcified, ancient thing, like a bullet left in his body.

Hours passed. Concho sat on the floor of his not-cell in the not-jail of the Caring Center under a colorful poster that pictured a loaf of sliced wholesome wheat bread, a clay pitcher of milk, and a glossy red apple, along with the words, "An Attitude of Gratitude", staring at the hair-tufted tops of his naked feet. Tired. His brain waves flat. His head pitched forward, arms turned out, bloodshot eyes gazing out of focus. Sometimes he would scratch a spot on one knee. But mostly he gazed, his mind drooping, sinking into a half-zone.

His bare feet reminded him of something. He slowly, mechanically pointed his retinas at them. Knobby toe-knuckles. Crooked toenails. What was it about his naked feet?

An indistinct memory of running. Thick vines swinging all around.

Out of weary curiosity, he took hold of an ankle and pulled his right foot toward his eyes, twisting it slightly to get a good look at the heel and the soft, white underpart of his foot.

Only it wasn't white. Not completely. In places the waxy arch was smeared green. Plant green. The oblong heel was stained an even darker green. Almost black. Odd.

He straightened that leg out and grabbed the other ankle, repeating the process.

Green. Chlorophyll green.

He let go of the ankle and leaned back, feeling as though he had picked up on something important. It took his addled mind a long while to wrap itself around the idea that perhaps this was the first clue, the first inkling of who he was. What he was all about.

He could still remember brief flashes of the dream. The one just yesterday morning when he was bolting through a humid, dense jungle. A voice at his back. A voice like a planet-sized wrecking ball. Throwing his arms up against thickets of broad, green leaves. Scrambling over moss covered rocks, looking down at his sock-less, boot-less, green-smeared feet.

Calling out her name. *Her* name.

Maybe if he concentrated hard enough—no—pressing his eyes shut he realized that trying to hold onto the dream was like trying to squeeze a wet bar of soap. Away it went. You had to let go and then the dream would return, you had to empty your mind. He voided all thought processes and gazed off into nothingness. Letting go.

Again, with more energy this time, he grabbed one of his ankles and pulled a foot around into view. He was on to something. Wait, what the hell was going on? His face squinted up, his mouth opened slightly.

Gone. The green stains had vanished. He angled the foot this way and that in the florescent light. The arches, the under-sides of the toes were now as white as bottom fish. White, waxy, unblemished.

Concho reached low and grabbed the other foot. Same story. The unmarked underbelly soles of a tenderfoot. The green was not there. His toes waggled whitely in the damp air of the not-cell. Who was doing this to him? Toying with him?

He leaned back against the metal bed, feeling like an ant caught in the gears of a mighty cosmic machine.

He didn't know who he was, where he was—except it was called Awareness, Missouri—or where he should be. Was he in the future, the past, or the present? How far would these hallucinations go?

A glass of mineral water sat on the floor next to him, a wedge of lemon perched on the transparent rim like a tropical leech.

He stared at it, knowing that somehow he needed to think. He needed to pull himself out of the gluey, primordial mud gumming up his thought processes.

He reached for the lemon, lifting it over his face, squeezing it with all his feeble strength.

"Awgh, ow, ouch," he growled as the acidic juice dripped into the cuts around his eyes, burned into the raw abrasions around his mouth.

He pressed the piece of fruit harder, draining the lemon. The juice coursed down his neck and chest finding more rips and tears.

"Gol-dang!" he cried, grabbing the mineral water, dashing it in his face.

Cold shock. The water seemed to blast through him, its fizz spreading the lemon juice deeper into the small wounds of his face and neck and chest. Concho jumped up and seized the bars of the not-cell. He panted and shook his head, sending out a silvery spray. His eyes sprang open.

The End Nears

"Mr. President," the vice president called out, knocking. He waited with his ear to the door. Again rapped a knuckle against the gray polyurethane door. "Mr. President, I really must insist that you come to the door."

"Go away," muttered a small voice on the other side.

The vice president, a lean, bland-faced politician in a navy blue suit turned and gave the four secret servicemen a raised eyebrow and an "at-least-we're-making-progress" look.

The square-headed secret servicemen stood shoulder to shoulder in dark suits, chewing gum with knobby jaw muscles.

"Steve," the vice president said, in a confiding tone, "the Oprah Rivera Springer shuttle is almost here. You agreed to this interview. Now, please if..."

The door slid open.

For the first time in weeks President Steven Panic made an appearance. He was wearing flannel boxer shorts and a white cotton t-shirt, revealing a thin neck and slack, stringy muscles in his arms and legs. A cigarette clung to his lips, the smoke forming a filmy question mark in the air. A lank of oily, graying hair hung down over his eyes.

"All right, come on in." he mumbled. "Not you," he said to the secret servicemen.

The vice president jerked at his crimson tie and stepped through the threshold. The president hit a button, causing the door to slide silently shut.

The president wandered across the spacious, cluttered bedroom to a wide portal overlooking the black neverendingness of outer space. He sat on the ledge of the portal, keeping his face toward the ocean-and-cloud covered Earth in the lower left corner.

"They bringing the booze?" the president asked.

"Yes."

"Good. I could use a martini." He took a long inhalation on the cigarette, and blew out yards of smoke. "And how's your wife? How's Angel?"

"Not much changed, really," the vice president answered, still standing, clasping his hands behind his back. "She'll be returning to Earth with the shuttle."

"You shouldn't be so hard on her," the president said. "She's the only realist in this damn mouse trap. Anyone who's not depressed as hell isn't paying attention."

"Steve," the vice president began.

"Phil," the president said, turning around, clenching his fists. "The whole planet is going to be destroyed. A million years of evolution wiped out. Everything civilization has worked for and all you and your goons care about is putting a happy face on it."

"You know we've been working on options. Nuclear warheads, uh, some kind of diversion scheme...this doesn't have to be the end."

The president stood for a moment in silence, staring at something on the floor about twenty feet away. His eyebrows snapped first up and then down. All at once he seemed to make a decision. He walked into a spacious closet filled with shoes on lighted racks, and neat rows of blue, black and charcoal suits.

"Phil, this is the end," the president called from the closet, pulling a black suit off the rack. "It's the end of everything. I want you to pull that stupid message you've been beaming down to the networks. That's the first thing."

"But it's actually improved your ratings. I mean it did until a couple weeks ago."

"Phil, wake up and smell the bullshit," he said calmly. "In a week, ratings won't even exist. Or if they do, God will be Nielsen... I'm *going* to make the announcement."

The vice president swiped his hand across his mouth. It was shaking. "Steve, I can't let you do that."

"You can't stop me."

"Steve, Jesus Christ, at least hold off for awhile. If the people have another week, give them that week. There'll be looting in the streets if you make that announcement."

The president buttoned the top button on a starched white shirt. "Good. Let them loot. Let them copulate in the streets if they want. Let them drink and smoke grass and dance naked and sing. Let them party like there's no tomorrow."

"But if I'm hearing you right, there is no tomorrow."

"Exactly," the president replied, bringing a smart knot to his tie, sliding it upward, tightening it with a practiced movement. "Tomorrows—like sugar to a diabetic—are a thing of the past."

"And that's what you're going to tell them?" the vice president asked, flabbergasted.

The president emerged from the closet transformed into his former self, dark tailored slacks, alligator shoes, white shirt, red tie. After swiping a comb through his hair, he almost looked like the paragon of Green Party Optimism who had won by a landslide in the last election. He daubed out his cigarette in an overflowing crystal ashtray and immediately pulled a new one out of a nearly empty pack of Marlborough reds. The president perched the cigarette in his lips, lit up and took a long, smiling drag and held it, looking mirthfully at the pasty-faced vice president.

He slowly let out a chest-full of smoke.

"Mmm," he growled pleasantly. "I like smoking. Don't you?"

"I don't smoke," came a crisp response.

"Never?"

The vice president shrugged quickly, hope for the future draining from his lanky frame. "I did a little at Yale."

"Did you inhale?" The president offered his pack. "Here."

The vice president looked at it with practiced disdain as the president shook the pack, continuing to offer it. Then he sighed and his face softened. "All right," he said, taking a cigarette, lighting up skillfully.

"It's like riding a bicycle," the president chuckled. "You never forget how."

The vice president exhaled, deliberately unrushed. "Yeah, that's pretty nice." Then stifling a cough and shaking his head, "It's been a long time." He took another cautious drag.

The two men sat at the edge of the wide port window, gazing out into space.

"It's still against the rules to smoke up here." the vice president said, a smile beginning to form around his eyes.

"Mmm-hmm," the president nodded, grinning, watching a tiny dark speck a long way off, moving almost imperceptibly toward the Cyrus One federal space station.

♌♌♌

"Tho, you're alive," said a cold-blooded voice from the shadowy corridor.

"DeBack? Is that you?" Concho asked. "Are you out there?"

Concho pressed his head to the bars, his eyes zipping from side to side, moving down the line of bars in the direction of the voice.

"DeBack?"

A second later a large, white, hair-covered man dressed in ripped mauve curtains stepped out of the darkness.

"Kenny Rogers?" Concho said, his face wrinkling with perplexity. Was this some kind of riddle? Another hallucination?

Then he realized that the huge man had a fat rattlesnake for a necktie.

"It'th me," DeBack said, his slice-of-pie head rising up beside the man's bearded face. A pink forked tongue flickered and recoiled back into the reptile's mouth.

"What, how?" Concho stammered as the large hairy man produced a ring of keys and began unlocking the not-cell door.

"We only have a few minuteth," DeBack said. "Look lively."

"But the guards?" Concho whispered.

"The guards go sleepy," the large man said, grinning.

"Who's this?" Concho asked the snake.

"Thith ith Bobby," DeBack answered, annoyed. "He wath, until rethently, a Englithh theep dog."

"English?" Concho eyed the new recruit suspiciously. "Oh, the sheep dog that was humping that old plaid footstool?"

"Yeth."

"Lovely."

Bobby blushed and gave a big toothy smile, too embarrassed to look up from fiddling with the lock.

"Did he eat. . .?"

"Yeth," DeBack said.

"But what happened to you?"

"Couldn't let them catch me, too. I found and ate the apple that fell out of the bag and rolled under the pilot'th seat. Then old Bobby here dithcovered my leather bag. He ate the lath apple."

Clack.

The door swung open and Bobby beckoned Concho to follow. Quickly, Concho pulled on a pair of socks and his cowboy boots.

The corridor was a long cement hallway lined with bright, graphically exciting posters highlighting the importance of the four food groups, fire safety, the dangers of second-hand cigarette smoke, everyone's duty to reduce fuel emissions, the joys of teenage celibacy, and masturbating. The not-cells on the opposite sides were identical to the one Concho was in, but all were empty. At the end of the long corridor, Bobby peered through the wire-mesh window on a steel door, his head moving this way and that, examining the next room.

He turned and grinned, a mouth crowded with teeth. "They still go sleepy time," he laughed.

Bobby shoved open the door, revealing a front office like that of a small police station. Two guards were slumped over desks, breathing heavily.

"What'd you do to them? Did Bobby knock 'em out?" Concho asked DeBack.

"We're not thavages." DeBack replied, offended.

"I know, but?"

"I bit them. Thlightly."

"Oh, great, so you just killed them a little." Concho said, nodding, alarmed, as though this finally confirmed a suspicion he'd been harboring about the snake.

Bobby guffawed. "He only bite a little," the dog man said, making a nibbling, teeth-clicking sound.

"I only gave them a thmall dose. I'm thaving my thtrength."

Concho swallowed back what he wanted to say, glared quickly at DeBack, and took in the remainder of the front office.

In one corner, a police radio crackled and whined. On the back wall in large brown letters against a speckled beige background were emblazoned the words, "The Caring Center." And underneath, "Awareness, Missouri, A Tradition of Heritage." Concho turned to DeBack, "These people are so, so..."

"Political?"

"Correct."

"What did you expect? Once a Puritan country, alwayth a Puritan country," DeBack said, swaying up and down to offset the joggling effect of Bobby's shoulder ride.

"Huh?" Concho asked.

Bobby opened the glass front doors, rustling the mauve curtains he wore in a rush of cold, moist air. Outside, the pale light of dawn was beginning to pastel the earth's eastern rim.

"Thith country, ath you know, was thettled in the sixteenth century by Puritanth," DeBack said, from his perch.

"Puritans?"

"Yeth. And they thet the standard. You think thith country was thettled by people who were perthecuted for their religion?"

"Well, yeah. Seems like the history books said so. Landed on Plymouth Rock," Concho said, wondering how he knew that.

DeBack rolled his beady eyes. "Nobody back in England cared about their religion. It'th just that the Puritanth couldn't throw a decent party."

Concho's brow furrowed up, jogging beside Bobby down the half-dozen front steps.

"It wath againth the law in thoth dayth to throw a bad party," DeBack said, his head bobbing up and down.

"How's that?"

Bobby indicated a small yellow car, himself climbing into the driver's seat. Concho settled into the passenger's side.

"Imagine," DeBack continued, sliding off Bobby's neck and onto the dashboard, "you've invited noblemen and their wiveth from the court over and you've thkimped on the food."

"Thkimped?" Concho asked.

DeBack frowned, curling up his fat body. "Yeth, you've thkimped on the food. You ordered the cheap cod and the two-day old herring, you therve a pig'th head, not the whole pig. You can't hold a dethcent conversation and then the muthician don't thhow up becauthe you forgot to pay them for the latht dig. Tho when everyone ith complaining and picking up their coatth and leaving, you try to cover it by telling them that your religion don't allow you to dance."

"Oh, I see."

"Of courthe the Puritanth were kicked out of England. And they were damn lucky that wath all they got."

"So you're saying America was..."

"I'm thaying America was thettled by party pooperth."

Concho held a blank look on his face. "Oh, I see."

DeBack looked away. "No you don't. Reach inthide my bag. It'th in back. There'th a spark plug. Pull it out."

Bobby backed the car out, veering, looking from rear view mirror to side mirror.

Concho steadied himself and felt around in the back until he located the mouth of the leather bag. His fingers ran randomly through the contents until his fingers curled around the hard, cold ceramic surface of the spark plug.

"Got it."

"Put the thkinny end in your mouth and clothe your eyeth."

"Where's this thing been?" Concho asked, examining the spark plug, remembering where he had to feed DeBack the second apple.

"Do it. Think of what you want to thee and you'll thee it."

Concho popped the spark plug halfway into his mouth and closed his eyes. Immediately colors and mists converged, like a lens at a movie theater coming into focus.

"You thee it?" DeBack asked.

"Yeah.." Concho rolled the spark plug to the side of his cheek and tried to speak clearly. "Thome real thtern-looking guy. Black hat. Black thuit. Riding in a buggy. Ith that hith wife and kidth with him?"

"Yeth."

"Hith wife lookth like Anthony Perkinth in a drethth. They're all thitting there like they got ramrodth up their... Hey!" Concho's eyes blinked opened and he pulled out the spark-plug-like thermometer. "What is this thing?"

"One of my little toyyh."

"Cool."

"You thaw the Puritanth."

"Yeah, but what does any of that have to do with this place?" he asked, gesturing around the clean, wide streets of Awareness.

"Thelf righteouthneththth. Itth been paththed down. It changeth form from one generation to the next. But the party pooperth are alwayth with uth. Jutht look around."

Concho nodded. He placed the spark plug back into his mouth and closed his eyes, making interested noises in the back of his throat.

"Thelf righteouthneththth ith alwayth an attempt to cover the fact that you don't know how to throw a good party."

Bobby got the car up to high speed and blasted through the empty streets. Health food stores and cappuccino stands whizzed past the car's windows without a sound.

Concho pulled the plug out and opened his eyes. "This car's awfully quiet."

"It'th electric," DeBack said, keeping an eye out the windshield. "Turn here," he snapped.

Bobby cranked the wheel hard, squalling around a corner, missing a light pole by inches, entering a street lined with town houses painted in a variety of muted, homeowner-association approved colors. Sandy earth tones.

"What'th the name of the thtreet?" DeBack asked.

Concho craned his neck. "Susan Sontag Avenue," he said.

"Okay," DeBack said. "We're on Thontag. Another couple blockth we take a hard right on Chopra and I think that getth uth back on Men Are From Marth, Women Are From Venuth Highway. That taketh us back out, doethn't it?"

Bobby nodded, then eyed the rearview mirror. "It would happen," he said.

"What do you mean it would happen?"

"We, we're being chased by pretty lights!" the dog man laughed, and floored the accelerator. "Put the petal to the metal," he howled. The needle on the speedometer stayed on 55. Regulated.

DeBack's head rose up, swaying from side-to side, looking out the back window. Concho swiveled around, peering around the head rest.

The street behind them was filled with dark blue minivans, their squad car lights dazzling out reds and blues. The sound of their sirens blasted through the early dawn.

The car lurched and swerved a hard left. DeBack sailed wildly across the dashboard, tangling around the steering column. Concho's head slammed against Bobby's large shoulder. The car filled with the dog man's yapping laughter.

"Chasing us!" he sang. "Chasing us!"

"I thaid take a right on Chopra!" DeBack cried, disengaging himself, slithering back up onto the dashboard. "Now where are we?"

Concho looked up, his head dodging around trying to catch a street sign through the blur of houses, trees, and lighted business signs. "This is Yanni. Yanni Boulevard."

"Yanni? Where the heck ith Yanni?" DeBack demanded, angrily exposing his slim, milky white fangs.

Suddenly the front window of the car was filled with flashing lights and minivans. Dozens of minivans. Minivans behind them were spreading out, filling both lanes. Gaining speed.

Bobby yipped and howled, pounding the steering wheel with an open palm.

DeBack was no where to be seen. Bobby hunched over the wheel weaving the car side to side, laughing, shouting, hooting.

"Let me have it," Concho demanded, grabbing one side of the steering wheel, pulling, straining.

Bobby looked over at him and lifted both woolly hands off the wheel. "Okay."

The car veered right, tilting up on two wheels. Bumping hard over a cement curb, it launched diagonally through a giant store front window that promised discounts on home entertainment systems. Huge shards of glass cascaded all around. Shattering, crashing noises exploding all about them. Bobby whooped and yipped with canine glee.

Inside the store, the car skidded, jolted, stopped. For a moment the world was silent. Concho kept his eyes closed and a scene slowly formed: Tall drooping trees, the dark-haired woman mouthing his name, sitting in a bed of rose petals. Then sirens.

Suddenly Concho realized the spark plug was back in his mouth and he spit it out. When had he stuck it back in? That spark plug could get to be an addiction. From outside he heard tires squealing and a convergence of police sirens. All Concho could see before him were televisions. A hundred—maybe more—television screens, toppled in every direction, two lying sideways on the hood of the car. All of them holding huge, close-up images of President Panic assuring Americans that the government was innovating new ways every day to guarantee a future filled with safety, bounty and lower taxes.

Concho heard a quiet giggle in the seat next to him.

Bobby leaned over with a big loony grin and whispered, "I've got a pecker!"

♌♌♌

Oprah Rivera Springer was the ultimate, if accidental merger. No longer entirely a man or woman. Nearly a woman. Well-nigh a man. Almost Hispanic. Somewhat African American, a bit Caucasian. Her/his existence was a miracle of modern medicine.

The event in Los Angeles had been billed as the marriage between the two most powerful elements in American Media: Talk Shows and The World Wide Wrestling Federation. They were all going to be represented there: Oprah, Geraldo, Jerry, Rosie, Montel and an entire TV Guide of pretend microphone jabbering baiters. The wrestling arena was packed. No holds barred, one long talkfest. Twenty cameras were poised to catch every grimace, every roll of the eyes. Microphones hung like spaghetti. The pay-per-view rights had been sold to E! for twenty-five million. A nation of trailer-parkers were poised on the edge of their tattered barcoloungers.

An earthquake rumbled right after the opening credits, and the nation watched in horror as the ceiling collapsed. A number of cameras remained red-lit as emergency crews rushed to rescue the treasured mouths of America's TV past from the twisted wreckage. Not one of the impersonators was saved intact. Instead, doctors worked for five days to assemble one ultimate, amalgamated host from the crushed remains of the many. Surviving limbs and organs were merged to produce one human being, and several careers and financial empires fused together. All on live television.

And Oprah Rivera Springer was born.

The resulting talk show host transcended sex, transcended ethnicity and got a bigger rating than anyone in fifty years of television. She/he was bigger than the Roseanne and Tom Arnold remarriage, performed by Reverend Jimmy Carter in Haiti. Bigger than the day England's King Freddie admitted to *Hard Copy* that he had cross-dressed all his life—wearing his mother's crown finally gave him away. Bigger, even, than the fact that a huge chunk of Southern California had fallen into the Pacific ocean and been towed by a super freighter to Japan.

The ultimate pay-for-view television event fusing the talk show hosts into one entity far outstripped the O.J. trial ratings. The new, improved Oprah Rivera Springer would be a walking Babel. Conservative Christian leaders shouted foul, evil, atrocious. Reversing the process of Eden where Man and Woman were created utilizing the materials of just one body is an abominable sin. The Pope angrily condemned the procedure, suspecting it would ultimately lead to a new form of birth control.

The five-day medical procedure was followed slice-by-dice, butterfly-stitch by butterfly-stitch by more than three billion horrified and fascinated paying viewers. When it was all over, Oprah Rivera Springer, outfitted in a long flowing white robe, appeared in a news conference and announced that as a result of the profits from the pay-for-view event she/he, he/she was buying a space shuttle and the Dominican Republic.

No one argued.

At 2200 hours, right on schedule, the gleaming white Op/Riv/Sprng shuttle eased into the Cyrus One docking port like a giant cruise ship. The technical staff burst into action at the dock site and in the central control room. Barometric pressure systems were connected. Seals were matched and suctioned into place. Air locks were tested and opened in a long series of hydraulic hisses.

A crowd of excited government workers and cabinet officials gathered in the official greeting center. Moments later, to the flashes of the official Cyrus One photographer's camera, Oprah Rivera stepped through a tall oval door and descended the red-carpeted steps into the space station's large, splendid greeting area. She/he wore a shimmering pale yellow robe, and a tall, vaguely Moroccan hat. His/her black mustache held a high gloss, glowing in the bright lights. Her/his dark cheekbones were skillfully highlighted. And the recent breast augmentation was apparent even under the loose garments.

The president in his dark suit stepped forward, greeting the talk show host with a warm, welcoming handshake.

The Oprah Rivera Springer entourage flowed into the greeting area, male and female assistants in neat tunics, followed by a few cameramen shouldering sleek black video cameras. Each was topped with a single white light like a glowing, hovering eye. The cameramen took up discrete positions, filming the historic meeting, the first of a celebrated TV personality and the U.S. president in outer space.

A military band played a brief, patriotic march as the president and Oprah Rivera Springer posed for a series of hand-clasped photos.

From earth, billions of people watched on TV.

♌♌♌

It was well past midnight at KAML, channel 37, a little UHF operation on the outskirts of the ancient city of Jerusalem.

A dark-haired intern in his late teens, Saleem, picked through the remains of an oily grain salad he was eating with a bent fork out of a cloudy Tupperware container. On the monitor in front of him he watched as the president of the United States made a few innocuous remarks about the significance of the occasion.

"Okay, okay," Saleem grumbled, "Let's get to the good stuff."

Like the rest of the planet, he couldn't get enough of Oprah Rivera Springer . The flowing robe. Individuals mixed. Some people were saying the fusion of the counterfeit, talk show hosts was the next step in human evolution. Others, including Saleem's aging, blind, one-tooth-in-her-head grandmother, decried it as a sign of the impending apocalypse.

Saleem sat with his fork poised, his eyes keen with interest as Oprah Rivera Springer took the microphone flanked with flags, and thanked the president and his staff for arranging the meeting.

A mention was made that after a brief commercial message and local station identification, the live interview would begin.

That was his cue.

Saleem hit a glowing yellow button on the large console and set into motion the broadcast of an ad for a local home security system, available to viewers in the Palestine region at a drastically reduced rate. On a second monitor, Saleem watched the satellite feed on Oprah Rivera Springer and the president settling themselves into comfortable arm chairs somewhere in Cyrus One. A woman with a camel-hair brush applied last-minute touches to the president's chin and jawline, while Oprah Rivera Springer was arranged and touched up by an array of assistants, tucking and smoothing the yellow robe, adjusting the angle of the Moroccan hat. Lip gloss was applied to his/her lips.

On the live monitor, Saleem checked the quality of a Burger King commercial. Dancing Whoppers. Singing shakes. French fries marching in formation. A man in a t-shirt and ballooning neon shorts addressed the screen in Arabic, urging viewers to indulge on behalf of Akbar, Inc.

Another typical night on Earth.

Saleem followed the Burger King ad with a station I.D.

A slide depicting salt formations on the shore of the Dead sea. A voice over, "You're watching KAML, channel 37, serving Israel, Jordan, Palestine and Syria."

Cut back to Cyrus One.

Oprah Rivera Springer touched her/his mouth with fingertips, looking wise and thoughtful.

"Mr. President, thank you for this first-ever live interview from outer space."

The president nodded.

The analogy of the famous talk show host leaned forward slightly, her/his face framed largely in the screen. The Moroccan hat tilted a few degrees starboard.

"Mr. President, I'd like to cut straight to the bone."

"Certainly."

"You and the executive wing of the government have been ensconced in space for months. Some would describe you as aloof. Others would say secretive. Many are more than a little suspicious. Can you set the record straight? Why have you taken to the space station in such a way?"

The president lit a cigarette and settled back in his chair. He inhaled, a long leisurely movement.

"Oprah Rivera Springer. I want to set the record straight all right. I want to clear up all the questions that have been floating around in the press, in the minds of Americans and other citizens of the world."

He tapped his cigarette into an off-camera ashtray.

"It has been written," the president continued, "that the truth shall set you free. And if that's the case, then I... what I have to announce should give everyone on earth an unprecedented sense of freedom."

"What are you saying?" Oprah Rivera Springer asked incisively, reaching up, fidgeting with the hat.

"What I'm saying is this," the president smiled grimly. "We felt the need to move into space based on the observations of a small group of NASA scientists. These scientists became aware of a grave danger to earth—they actually knew about it as far back as 1997. An object in outer space is headed for a direct hit with earth."

"The asteroid?" she/he asked. "But we were told it would miss by—"

"At the time it was spotted, it was not clear that its orbit would impact the earth. In fact it was extremely difficult to study because its path took it directly between the earth and our sun. It would be as if someone on the surface of the sun were to shine a spotlight toward earth. Would we see it clearly? Not likely."

The president wrapped one leg over another and continued. "Our NASA science team recently spotted the asteroid just before it passed in front of the sun. It was a brief sighting and quite frankly there was some speculation as to the real trajectory of its path. Now, I'm told it *is* confirmed. This very large object of rock and iron *will*—I emphasize *will*—impact the earth in days."

Oprah Rivera Springer flipped through pages of notes. The Moroccan hat slipped forward and fell from her/his head to the floor. "What... uh... the impact," Oprah Rivera Springer stammered, barely able to speak. Sheets of notes slid off his/her knees. She/he looked around wildly, as if for help from the cameramen.

Finally, she/he said in a quavery voice, "What kind of damage are you, uh, we, expected to incur? To absorb?"

"We're talking about very, very widespread damage. No, let me be perfectly honest," the President said. "Politicians are trained to put a gloss on things of this nature and this kind of gloss runs counter to my entire life's upbringing." One hand gestured in empty air.

"I understand."

"Yes, well, I am very sorry to have to announce that human life will be—uh—annihilated." His face grimaced, a frowning, fist-like expression. "Completely annihilated."

The camera cut to a reaction shot of her/his trembling, eyes widening slightly, mustache quivering.

"First," the president continued, "the impact alone will level every standing building. In fact, one geologist I spoke with, in Texas, speculates that the impact could open a crack running all the way to the planet's center, bringing up a flood of magma and liquid heavy metals from the earth's core. Without question, the atmosphere will be choked with dust and debris, covering the Earth in an opaque blanket if it hits land, and flooding the earth if it hits water. The sun will be completely blotted out. The weather will change dramatically. And a second ice age may ensue that will make the first one look like a schoolboy's snowball fight."

"You're saying?" she/he asked.

The president cleared his throat. "I'm saying that for the next millennium—in the words of C.S. Lewis—it will be always winter and never Christmas."

♌♌♌

No one spoke. The men in denim shirts who had hustled out of the squealing minivans with guns drawn now stood in the wrecked home entertainment store before a pyramids of TV sets, watching with mouths agape at the president's apocalyptic announcement. The only sound was of glass clinking and cracking as the men shifted from one foot to the other, beginning to look askance at each other. What now?

This changed everything.

"Friends." The voice was somewhere between an alto and a tenor. "Don't despair."

The men turned. Concho noticed DeBack whispering in Bobby's ear. He strained to see who the voice belonged to. Their ranks split and a strange vehicle—half all-terrain and half golf cart—crunched over the broken glass.

Sister Gaia was huge. She filled the entire contraption, and then some, flesh flowed over the sides of the vehicle like oozing volcanic lava. She fit the description of the Goodyear blimp and the circus fat lady, all rolled into one.

"Remember, this is the same government that has been telling you that taxes were going to go down, services up, and you were free to pursue your own happiness."

"But, Sister Gaia..."

Concho craned his neck further out the window.

"Gentlemen, if the world is going to end, so what? How should that change the way you live, what you do? Do you want more sex, more food? One more football game? An extra shot of whiskey, a bottle of great red wine?"

"But, we'll at least need to facilitate a dialogue with our family members and loved ones," one man announced in a shocked voice, "before the asteroid hits."

She waved an arm, causing another lava flow of flesh underneath it.

"To what end? Are they going to understand something that is currently not understandable? No." She smiled bigger than the man in the moon. "Yes, go home. But when you've done your work here. The way to save the world is *not* to panic, *not* to change anything."

The others murmured in agreement.

"You were going to arrest these pornographic criminals. right?"

"Yes, Sister Gaia," a moronic chorus sang out.

"Then go ahead and do it."

The men turned to face the car. Concho sighed, leaned back in the seat. He glanced over to Bobby...who wasn't there.

"Where's...?"

"Ssssh," came a voice from the back seat.

"Come on out with your hands up."

"Aw shit, DeBack. I'm getting very, very tired of these clowns."

"Come on out or we'll shoot," Rick the coordinator, called, sighting down the barrel of his gun. He had obviously missed his latest Twelve-Step Anger Anonymous meeting.

An alto/tenor scream rent the air. The ATV-Golf Cart spun around, engine roaring, tires squealing.

Above the noise, Concho heard Bobby's voice and Sister Gaia's laughter.

"I've got a pecker!" he shouted, his arms around Sister Gaia as they drove over the hill and out of sight. "I've got a pecker, and it's just for you!"

The caring-nurturers of Awareness, Missouri took off on foot after their Queen Philosopher and her pornographic abductor.

Concho pulled his bruised body from the little electric car, straightened up and wandered outside. The morning sun brightened the sky as it had for millions of years. He searched the wide blue expanse of the firmament overhead, searching for something, some sign that...

Yes. There it was. An enormous dot hanging in the heavens just to the right of the sun. A celestial period looking for a complete sentence.

He sat down heavily on a large man-made rock of cement, in a small garden terrace that was meant to beautify the street. His fingers trailed aimlessly through the sandy soil, doodling circles within circles.

This is what he had seen with DeBack's false eyelash two days ago. A dark head followed by a tail of dusty vapor. A sperm swimming through space toward its one and only egg called Earth.

"Everything that ith going to happen hath already been written. You theee?" a voice hissed to his left.

Concho looked over and sighted DeBack curling, climbing, through the branches of a thorny bush.

Concho let out a long, weary sigh. "What'd you say?"

"It'th all been written," DeBack repeated.

"In your cave, you mean?"

"Maybe, and in other placeth."

"Such as?"

DeBack grimaced up at the sky. "Take thith athteroid for example."

"What about it?"

"Predicted."

"By who?"

"By whom," he corrected. "In the Book of Daniel."

"You are the churchiest damn snake I ever met."

DeBack continued. "The King of Babylon, Nebuchadnezzar, had a dream in which he thaw a large thtatue. The thtatue of a king. The head wath made of gold, the chest of silver, the thtomach of brath, had legth of thteel and feet of iron and clay."

"Kinda like my feet right now."

DeBack crackled through the dry leaves of the bush. "The king wath confuthed by thith until old Daniel cometh in and interpretth the dream. Thays the head of gold reprethentth Nebuchadnezzar and Babylon, and that the cheth reprethentth the kingdom that will come after him, the thtomach the kingdom after that and tho forth."

"Yeah, so."

"Tho the thtatue reprethentth political hithtory from Babylon to the prethent day. The feet of clay could be theen ath the U.N., or the attempt at a global economy."

"So what's the asteroid connection?"

"Can I finithh?"

"Sorry."

"And the dream endth with a rock, unhewn by human handth, hurtling from out of nowhere and thmathhing the thtatue to dutht," he said with a slowly twisting smile.

Concho let a line of dry, limey soil slip through his fingers.

"And the dutht," DeBack said, "is carried away on the wind never to be theen again."

Concho gulped at what moisture was left in his throat, looking up at the black dot in the sky.

"Says that, huh?"

"Yep."

"In the Bible?"

"Book of Daniel. Chapter two."

Concho let out a prolonged sigh. "Is that on your cave wall too? The asteroid hitting the...the earth?"

"Did you thee it?"

"Well, no."

DeBack gave a kind of shrug.

"It's *your* cave!"

"I'm buthy. Got a lot of thingth to do. Bethideth, you thaw how hard it wath to thee the future in my cave."

The end of the world was beginning to fray Concho's nerves. There were so many unanswered questions floating around. "How the hell does a snake know to fly airplanes?" he groused. "And know about TV and CDs and—Jed Clampet?"

"Jed Frigging Clampet."

"Whatever."

"Don't mithquote me."

"Just answer the dang question." Concho stood up. The early heat of the day was pressing in around him, boiling like his temper. A blue bottle fly whizzed around his face, dive-bombing his mouth.

"Concho..."

"And why in God's name are we going to Washington, D.C. to survive a asteroid? Tell me that. That one's really got me bamboozled. You know..." Concho paced into the roadway, then whirled back and demanded, "I mean, shouldn't we be back at your cave with a bunch of canned food and maybe some TV dinners and..."

"Concho," DeBack said, his voice lowered.

Concho stamped his feet on the asphalt. "We could find us some babes and ride this thing out."

DeBack's eyes were level, intense, "Concho...Get my bag."

"What?"

"Get my bag. We don't have much time."

Concho started toward the crashed minivan, then whirled around, "What am I? Some kind of servant? Is that why you conjured me?"

"Go on, go on," DeBack coaxed.

Concho frowned, turned and reentered the store. "Probably be better off wherever I was before you conjured me," he muttered, then returned and lifted DeBack over one shoulder.

"Which one looks good to you?" DeBack asked, swiveling his head from one minivan to the next.

"That one," Concho said, indicating one at the outer edge of the bunch. "But won't it make us an easy to target?"

"If anyone doeth notice, they won't care. All betth are off. Nothing ith the thame. All prioritieth have changed."

"I guess you're right. I feel kinda sick."

Concho opened the driver's side door, and tossed in the bag. He took a moment to lay DeBack into the seat next to him and to check the dashboard. The motor was already running so he climbed behind the wheel.

"You do know how to drive?" DeBack asked.

"Yeah, way better than you know how to fly an airplane," he said, pulling the van into reverse, carefully, then into drive, slowly making their way down the empty streets.

"So what're we gonna do?"

"What do you mean?"

"You can't just stay a snake. If that damn dog hadn't eaten that last apple..."

DeBack coiled upon the seat, raising his head to see over the dashboard.

"And what's going to happen to Bobby?" Concho asked.

"He'll change back into a dog when he paththeth all of the apple from hith body. Which meanth..."

"That Sister Gaia's going to get caught doing naughty, naughty with an Old English Sheep dog," Concho laughed.

DeBack laughed too, his head waving around like a blind Blues singer.

"But she seemed really smart and nice."

"It won't hurt her reputation. In fact it might change her whole outlook on thingth."

"So, what do we do now?"

"There'th one left," DeBack said.

"One more apple? Where?"

DeBack hummed an unhappy affirmative. "It wath stolen from me a long time ago."

"Where's it at?"

DeBack didn't reply.

"Where's it at?"

DeBack's fat body rippled with movement, uncoiling until he stretched out more fully.

"What's wrong? You scared or something? Let's go get it back!" Concho said.

"It'th at Heaven'th Gate."

"You mean...?" Concho stared at him. "Up in..." his thumb jerked skyward.

"No," DeBack said. "Not up in heaven. I mean the theme park, Heaven'th Gate. It'th a holy roller amuthement park in Virginia."

"A what?"

"The right, Reverend Raymond Friend, he'th a TV preacher. Runth a Chrithtian theme park in Virginia."

"Not another evangelist."

"If we're lucky we won't meet him."

Concho drew the minivan to a stop at a four-way. "Which highway takes us outa here?"

"Men Are From Marth."

Concho checked the green street signs that hung from the lamp posts, put on his blinker and took a left. "So," he chuckled, "This Reverend Friend stole one of your apples?"

"Yeth."

"He wandered away from a group of nature worthhiperth, got lost near my tree. He took an apple."

Concho laughed. "What'd he do with it? How do you know it still exists?"

"He'th got a museum. Dithplayth thingth like gopher wood from Noah'th ark, a feather from the wing of the angel who wrethtled with Jacob, thplinterth of wood from the crothth, thtuff like that. Courth, not any of them the real thing."

"And an apple from the snake in the garden."

"Mmm-hmm. My apple ith the only real magical thing there."

"Out-snaked the snake!" Concho chortled merrily.

DeBack reached out with his rattle and twisted a knob on the radio. "Let'th see what the Cronkiteth have to thay about all thith."

Every channel carried the ongoing live interview with President Panic and Oprah Rivera Springer .

♌♌♌

Saleem crawled around the floor under the console cleaning up the tabouli salad he'd dropped, the voice of his grandmother swimming around in his head. The end. The apocalypse.

With the last of the salad whisked back into the Tupperware, he slid back in his chair, his mind crackling, his synapses firing away, thoughts going in every direction.

The phone rang.

"KAML, serving Israel, Jordan," Saleem answered, glad for a small, normal gesture.

Mr. Karamesh, the station manager, was calling from his suite in Tel Aviv. "You getting all this on tape?" he demanded in a gruff voice.

"Yes, sir. Yes, sir, of course."

"Good."

The phone clicked on the other end.

Saleem held the receiver a moment longer, a feeling of the ridiculousness spiraling around inside his mind. What would a tape matter now? What did any of it matter? Everything would be over in a week.

The moment he returned the receiver to its cradle, the phone burst out in another ring. Saleem lurched back, letting out a cry.

"Hello?"

"Saleem?" an excited female voice asked.

"Yuh-yes. Yes. This is Saleem, you've reached KAML."

"Saleem! It's Leah."

"Leah!"

"I don't have much time. I'm on Dr. Pitter's satellite phone."

"Yes?" Saleem relaxed at the sound of Leah's voice. Emotions played back images of the two weeks they'd spent together before she'd gone to the dig near the Dead Sea. The brief kiss near the Wailing Wall. The day visiting the market. The feel of her cool hand in his. The film they'd seen at...

"Saleem!"

"Allah Kabar, it's so good to hear from you," he said. "I got your letter a week ago, but with everything that's happening, I haven't had time to answer it."

"Forget the letter. I have big news," she said over the crackle of the phone. "Big. News."

"Did you hear about the asteroid?" he asked.

"Yes," she said hurriedly, "I've known about it for some time. Mother told me before she and dad boogied into space. But I've got a scoop for you, Saleem. A scoop! You can break this story to the rest of the world!"

"Leah, are you crazy? The world ends in a week! No one's gonna listen to some news from an archeological dig that..."

"Saleem, listen to me. This is bigger than the..." There was a loud crackling on the line. "Can you hear me? This is bigger than the asteroid!"

"How...?" he began, but had to hold the phone away from his head, as a brain-tweaking, high-pitched whine reeled out of the phone.

"Saleem!" he heard Leah shout over the interference. "I'll call you again, first thing in the morning."

The phone went dead. He looked from the phone back to the monitor, where a stunned, weepy Oprah Rivera Springer was lighting up one of the president's cigarettes.

"Is there nothing we can do?" she asked him.

"We've got a rocket armed with the largest neutron bomb ever assembled that will be launched at just the right moment...but..."

"But?"

"The scientists don't think it will do anything more than add fuel to the fire, so to speak."

The talk show host winced. "No hope, huh?"

Panic shook his head. "An asteroid is a heavenly body. It would seem this is destined."

"After the asteroid hits, I guess you and the other chosen few will ride it out up here?" Oprah Rivera Springer said.

The president nodded. "Yes, but we can't last forever. We're dependent on food and other supplies from Earth. We have perhaps another two months of food and water."

"Then what?"

The president shrugged. "I prefer not to think about it."

Oprah Rivera Springer leaned back looking frazzled, shaky. The cigarette she/he held trembled out a small rain of black ash from the tip.

"Don't you feel that the captain should go down with the ship?" the newly built talk show host asked.

"I'll admit," said the president, "that from a very human standpoint our first thoughts were of self-preservation. But quickly it became clear that it was not a possibility, and that we in Cyrus One had a greater purpose. I gave a directive several months ago that this space station should become a floating memorial to the human race. For the past few months we have assembled videos, books on CD, facsimiles of ancient manuscripts and so forth, that document for all time to any future space voyagers the story of the human race. It is my hope that we will not be forgotten."

Tears welled up in Oprah Rivera Springer's mascared eyes. "Is there a record of Oprah Rivera Springer?"

The president nodded. "Certainly. No story of our species would be complete without you."

"Thank you," she/he whispered, wiping tears out of her/his eyes and moustache. "That means so much."

Saleem struggled to his feet. His thin body felt as if it was full of wet sand bags. As the interview continued playing out on the monitor, he made his way out of the control room, brushing through a steel side door and out into the huge Mediterranean night where the cool air smelled sweet and clean. He slowly walked around the perimeter of the small brick building set on a hill above Jerusalem. At the front entrance he propped his laden body against his bicycle. He could see the street lights of the city below, the moving lights of late-night taxis. Everything looked so normal. So beautifully and tenderly ordinary. So why...if this thing...his thoughts raced against each other, forming nothing in particular. Only a vague sensation of dread.

At first he could only hear a soft breeze rustling over rocks and sand. Then he heard something else, an ancient sound that caused his fingers to dig into the front tire of the bicycle. From far off, somewhere in the heart of the ancient city of Israel, he heard a wail. A thin, calling voice crying out against the doom. The hurtling apocalypse.

After a second the lone voice was joined by another. And another. A growling chorus of despair rising up from a planet where another species found itself headed for extinction.

♌♌♌

"Give me a break," DeBack muttered, switching off the radio with his tail. "Oprah Rivera Springer ain't even a comma or a dangling partithiple in the heather of humanity." The snake looked with disapproval out at the trees and little white batten board houses and rolling hills whizzing past the windows.

Concho hadn't been listening. His thoughts marched forward in a different direction. "Here's what I don't get," he said. "Okay. Our plane crashed through an apartment house in the middle of this utopian community and there was that guy with the Chinese lantern over his privates and those two women with the mayonnaise or something, then that woman in the bathtub with fish and those kids smoking crack and yet you say these folks are Puritans. Or some new version of Puritans."

"Puritanth are only Puritan on the outthide."

Concho thought about this and other questions that plagued him. He was pleased that he had caught DeBack in an answering mood.

"Okay, so tell me this," Concho blurted, "I know about the asteroid and about you and the apples and all. But there's something I still don't get. Why're we going to Washington, D.C.?"

DeBack slipped slowly off the passenger seat, slithered his fat length between the front seats and stretched out on the bench seat in back. "Ithn't it enough to know that your life may be thpared?"

"Well, yeah. That's pretty good to know. But let's get real. You're the snake in the garden. You invented lying."

"I rethent that."

"I didn't think it'd make you happy."

Concho continued driving, waiting for a response. There was rustling in the back as though DeBack were settling in.

"I told you that everything hath been written."

"Right."

"What happenth next ith altho written."

"You're being cloudy."

"The thingth in my cave...The darknethth of the future continueth to thcroll forward ath the yearth go on. The fact that you were able to thtumble around and get yourthelf lotht back there, then make it back out tellth me that the world will continue to be."

"The *world* is going to continue because I got lost in your cave." Concho said, jumping on that particular detail.

"That'th what I think."

"The *world* is going to continue, but will *people*? Hmm? What if only animals are going to continue? Say...oh, I don't know...snakes for example."

"Did you thee my cave ath a hithtory of thnaketh? How many thnaketh did you thee?"

"Don't change the subject, DeBack. You may think I'm some dumb hillbilly numb-nuts, but buddy, you need me. You need me to drive this van. You need me to get you to Washington. Now if this is gonna be some kinda partnership, then you better start cutting me in."

A spout of anger gushed from the back. "Can thith wait!" the snake roared. "Can we just get that apple back, firtht?

"It'th pretty hard for me to talk with thith thtupid thplit tongue," he sputtered.

Concho nodded, driving, allowing DeBack to cool down to the sound of the tires droning over the pavement. "Okay," he said. "But you gotta promise me, you'll fill me in when you're a man again. I mean, this is a once in a lifetime thing. I got this immortal talking snake here in the car with me and I got one or two questions on my mind. And I don't just mean stuff like Washington, D.C. either. I mean things like history. How time works. Stuff like that. Okay? Who knows? I might want to write a book about it someday."

Silence from the back. Sullen, brooding, go-away-and-leave-me-alone silence.

"Okeeee-Dokeee?" Concho pressed.

"Yeth, yeth, okay already."

♌♌♌

"Look, there's a new one. Looks like..." The vice president peered out the observation window, "...University of Iowa, maybe."

President Panic tapped the ash from his cigarette onto the floor. "Jesus, that's my alma mater."

"And there's another."

"What's that one say?"

"Pretty simple. It says B-A-S-T-A-R-D-S."

"Sign them up. I'm going to need new speech writers. If we get out of this alive."

Williams stared at the President. He had become impenetrable, untouched by the asteroid or criticism. Colleges and municipalities all over the globe had taken to spelling out messages to the inhabitants of Cyrus One on clear days. Some of the messages were simple like: "C-O-W-A-R-D-S!" (Oscar Wilde University, outside of London), or the elegant "P-U" from Penn. One corporate plea was particularly touching: "DON'T LEAVE HOME WITHOUT US." Didn't the president understand that going out this way was...

"Stop it, Phil. Judgment is written all over your face. Jesus, it's tiresome."

He dropped the cigarette on the floor and crushed it with his moccasin. "No wonder..." His voice trailed off and he kept his eyes on the observation window.

"No wonder Angel's leaving?" Phil said, finishing the president's statement. He stepped forward, his fists balled. "You dumb pipsqueak. Bad enough we're considered the ultimate cowards, but now with that Oprah Rivera Springer creature, we've become a sideshow."

"She/he is quite a tasty dish, as a matter of fact." The president looked at his nails. "Not unlike sweet and sour chicken, if you get my drift."

"Ugh, you disgust me." Williams' eyes were inflamed.

Panic spread his hands. "Well, it's not as grand as Kennedy and Marilyn but, given the circumstances, it was the best I could do."

"God, you make me sick." Williams lip curled. "I've hated you since I first laid eyes on you as a congressman."

Panic assumed a defensive position. "Didn't stop you from sucking up to me for the vice presidency, did it, Mr. High-and-Mighty Moral Majority?"

His face purple, Williams swung with all his might at Panic, who ducked, clumsily. The two went crashing into a console, just as a long tendril of cold smoke seemed to reach out from the asteroid.

Straight toward Cyrus One.

♌♌♌

Even though it was midmorning with the sun slowly climbing toward noon, the highway was strangely empty. The landscape all around was tranquil, green postcard-like, like any other day, yet time seemed to stand still. In an hour they had passed no more than one motorcycle, an army truck and three slow-moving cars. When he mentioned this to DeBack, the snake replied sleepily:

"What do you expect? They think the world'th coming to an end."

"I guess I sorta figured on everyone running around. Going nuts."

"Where're they going to run to?" the snake asked.

"I don't know. I'd be tempted to high-tail it someplace."

"Like?"

"Like to your cave. Some place underground. I don't know exactly."

"Didn't you hear?" DeBack said. "The Texath geologitht thaid that there would be a thplit in the earth. All the way to the core."

Concho shook his head. "I just don't see how you and me are supposed to ride this out. I mean, when everyone and their dog might bite the dust."

"Do you conthtantly have to bring that up?"

"You know, come to think of it, you said everyone gets reincarnated. So does that mean that if everyone dies they'll all go to heaven?"

Concho glanced at the rearview mirror, reaching up and adjusting it so he could see DeBack lazing in the back seat.

"I didn't thay that."

"You kinda did though. You said that in between lives everyone gets a breather."

"That'th not the thame as heaven."

"Okay, okay. Don't play word games with me."

"There'th a differentth?"

"All right. I'll rephrase everything then." Concho let out a long, exaggerated sigh, shifting in his seat. He felt like a trial lawyer facing a particularly persnickety judge. "If the asteroid hits and everyone dies, won't that kinda crowd things up in the afterlife?"

"No."

"No?"

"You don't underthand how it all workth."

"You're right about that, I don't understand. That's why I'm asking, dumb ass." Rolling his eyes, tapping out a Morse code of impatience on the steering wheel.

"I'm under no obligation to anthwer any quethtion."

"And I'm under no obligation to help you!" Concho cried out.

"You don't have to athk me about the afterlife, Concho. You've been there, I haven't. I have never died. I have alwayth lived from the beginning of the world. All I know ith that everyone getth a breather, like I thaid. For all I know, everyone living will be reincarnated ath cockroacheth."

"So you're saying you don't know."

"Correct."

"Well why didn't you just say so then?"

"Jutht drive."

"No can do."

"Why not."

"We're running outa gas. Check the gauge if you don't believe me."

"Then thtop and get some gath."

"You got any cash, nature boy? Got any pockets in that snake skin of yours?"

Muttering curses against all reptiles, Concho turned to search the roadside for a gas station, a sign, anything that would give them a chance to pull off and...

A sharp pain in the back of his neck. Twin pricks of pain first breaking the skin, then needling deeper into the muscle in his neck. Twin hot spots flared deep in the tissue and a hot, sliding sensation traveled up his neck, spreading into his head.

He twisted around slowly, feeling dizzy and ill. He turned in time to see DeBack retracting his fangs, settling back into the seat.

"Yuh...yuh bit me!" Concho's voice sounded slow and dull and distant, like a cassette player losing power, *"Yuuuuuugghhh — biiiiiiggghhhht — meeeaaagghhh."*

"I thhould have done that two dayth ago," DeBack said across a chasm of time and space.

"Yuh bit me."

Concho's brain felt as if it was expanding, like he had been an ant living in what had been an external, black, canvas night, only now the ceiling of the world was rising up above him, away from him in all directions, lifting, becoming a giant circus tent, a brand new billowing dimension he had never dreamed existed. His gray matter felt like an enormous, supernatural cavern now lit in misty colors, filled with moving shades.

"Enough of thith bickering, mortal. Find a gath thtation. Get thome fuel and get uth to Heaven'th Gate and then to Wathington, Dee. Thee."

Concho turned and stared glassily at the road ahead.

"Did you hear me?"

"Yes." Concho's eyes were fixed on the windshield.

"Find fuel. Yeth, DeBack. Anything you thay, DeBack." The snake curled up. A slow chuckle rattled from the back of the small blue minivan. "Forgot who you were dealing with, didn't you?"

Concho blinked back wave after wave of cloudy nausea, as though his stomach was full of a mixture of goat cheese and urine. He swallowed back a dry, lumpy feeling in his throat and ran a hand across his damp forehead. He also had the sensation of flying and gripped the steering wheel with all his might to assure himself of his groundedness.

Up ahead, nestled among wiry mimosa trees and telephone poles, a gas station appeared. An ancient, rusted-out junkyard of dismantled cars and piles of no-good tires had been dumped to one side of the station.

"Pull in here?" Concho asked in a voice dry as sawdust.

DeBack's head rose up to get a view over the dashboard. "Yeth. Thith will be jutht fine."

Concho wheeled into the gas station. The van's tires crackled over reddish gravel and jounced through minor potholes in the decades-old asphalt. The vehicle halted beside two stark, rust-washed fuel pumps, the sort usually displayed in museums dedicated to whimsical early twentieth century America.

Through an eight-paned window, the pimpled teenage station attendant rose resentfully, curling up an issue of *Naked Nazis* and swatting at a mosquito on his forehead. A moment later, the attendant's large face appeared at the van's window.

"What can I do yuh for?" the kid asked, removing the wet remains of the insect squashed just under the bill of his *It Ain't Easy Being a Sex Symbol* cap.

"Um..." Concho began. He hesitated, trying to clear his mind enough to say what he wanted.

The attendant flubbed his lips, scratched at the two-day beard on his red, bumpy face. "Take yer time."

"F-fuel," Concho managed.

"F-fuel? You mean guh-gas?" the attendant mimicked.

"Yes," Concho gasped, his eyelids fluttering.

"You want ruh-regular or suh-suh-super?"

"Thuper," a voice commanded from somewhere in the back.

The Attendant bent forward slightly. "Thuper?" he responded. "Did thomeone thay th-th-th-thuper?"

Concho swallowed deeply. "Yeah."

The attendant snickered maliciously, sauntered to the back end of the van and spun off the gas cap.

As the pump nozzle clattered into place, Concho leaned back and tried to turn his head back toward DeBack, but his neck muscles were too stiff. "How're we suppose to pay for this?"

"Juth drive off."

"But...?"

"You will drive off."

"'kay."

Concho settled back against the seat, still clutching the steering wheel. He hadn't eaten in two days and he was weak, but the thought of food sounded about as inviting as sucking a wad of hair out of a shower drain.

He sensed the snake's poison traveling through his body's pipe system of veins and arteries, fanning out into the millions of capillaries. The skin on his hands turned maroon.

The gas station attendant's face sprang back into view.

"That's gonna be s-s-s-sixteen-fifty."

Concho stared forward, as though locked in to position.

"You deaf?" the kid persisted. "Sixteen-fifty."

Concho started the van, revved the engine, inched forward.

"Hey, you bastard," the kid hollered, following alongside.

Concho turned, drew back a fist and popped the gas station attendant in the mouth.

The kid reeling backwards landed on his butt, feet straight up in the air.

Tires squealed. Gravel and dust flew. And the sound of a snake's laughter filled the air and gradually receded into the distance.

♌♌♌

Angel Williams slipped into a pair of boot-cut jeans and, sitting on the edge of the narrow bed, pried on a pair of black ankle boots. She stood to look in the full-length mirror. Tugged at the loose-fitting black silk blouse. Hmm. Not bad for a woman in her early 40s who'd given birth four times. Plus the miscarriages, eight pregnancies altogether. She'd proved so fertile that her second husband rarely availed himself anymore of the marital chores he'd once been so enthusiastic about. Her last miscarriage had taken place soon after the vice president's vasectomy. The OB/GYN at Walter Reed could only shake his head.

Angel turned sideways in the mirror. Grimaced. Patted the tummy that pouched out just slightly. Damn. Living in space did funny things to your body. Irritatingly funny. Not ha-ha funny.

Nevertheless her olive skin looked great against the black silk. The whole effect was pleasingly un-second ladyish. Less like Beltway blah and more Italian *Vogue*. The mantel of a politician's wife had rested uneasily on Angel's shoulders. She'd always approached it like an actress preparing for a role, Morgan Fairchild in a made-for-TV movie. She could smile for the camera like the rest of them. Make sparkling conversation at $500-a-plate fund raisers. She had even allowed her hairstyle to be reworked for public life. During the campaign her unruly shoulder-length tresses had been snipped into an unremarkable, impersonal helmet, giving the impression of one who had better things to do than fret over her bangs. The change in coif made the round of women's magazine covers and inspired a national debate over glum -vs- workaday styles for the professional female. Most pundits came out in favor of the new "do," symbolic, they said, of a Wild Child coming of age, handing in the badge of rebellious youth.

In the mirror she saw that at long last the government-issued hairstyle had grown back into the lavish mane of dark curls she'd always loved.

Now she saw the person who had lived on the inside all those years, that earthy, tacky, real-worlder who loved dinosaur rock like The Doors, frozen pizza, and sweat shirts. It felt good. A moment of ecstatic reawakening.

And it felt great to be getting back to Earth. She missed the little things. The way sunlight makes your skin feel like it's glowing. The shouts of children on a playground. Cold air making her teeth ache. The sound of automobile tires on wet pavement. Milk out of the carton. Humidity. Dirt.

She missed dirt. The feel of it. The comforting, organic smell of it after a night of rain. The alarming contrast of green blades of springtime grass emerging from the dark earth.

Buck Rogers. Flash Gordon. Star Trek. Star Wars. All the movies made space seem so sleek, hip, radiant. But the *ideas* of space were much more exciting than the day-to-day drudgery of it.

Truth is, it was like being stuck on a very small, metallic *Gilligan's Island.* Everyday the same idiotic bureaucrats, the same corridors, the same view of the same stars. Lately, of course, you could see the asteroid in its race toward earth. A sperm swimming toward a bloated ovum. But that had been the only change in months. Otherwise the air in the space station was so dry her sinuses hurt. The steel flooring made her arches ache. Artificial gravity gave her diarrhea. And the drinking water—God—with every gulp you knew it was the same H_2O you'd flushed with last night's liquid colonic outburst.

She wanted to experience Earth again. Even if it was only for a week. Life on the space station had not been good for her. In the first week all her plants died. Something about the dry air. Then the artificial plants had faded and bleached out when placed too close to the portals. Something about invisible rays and cosmic particles. "Harmless to humans." Uh-huh. Then her appetite had vanished. Normally a big eater, she'd been reduced to nutrition capsules. And still she gained weight. Why couldn't you just gain weight in your breasts?

At least she hadn't had to wear a bra up here.

Then the nightmares began. Running from a black, nameless nemesis. Screaming in her sleep, terrifying the aides. On waking she seemed to be surrounded by the smell of decay, death. She brushed her teeth several times a day, bathed endlessly. And still the scent of rot swirled all around her, coming out of the walls, swirling out of open doorways. Eventually, after the onboard psychiatrist covertly circulated a damning report on her mental condition, the president's chief-of-staff had quarantined her to this wing. Later, her prison had become this room, a 24 x 24 cubicle formerly used as a storage space for unclassified documents. Members of the executive staff had cleared out the files and brought in a narrow bed, dressing table, a TV and a bookshelf. Food brought in on a tray by her husband, who looked embarrassed and beaten. But the room still retained its aura of clerical efficiency, a back closet where unnecessary, outdated objects were stored.

Yes, she was ready for the return to Earth, even if it meant an early, catastrophic death. Better than this slow eating away, this dying by degrees.

"Mrs. Williams," a voice said from the overhead speaker.

Angel jumped. Then smiled to herself. "Yes?"

"Mrs. Williams, the shuttle disembarks at 0700 hours."

She glanced at the digital clock near her narrow blue-green sheeted bed. The large orange numbers spelled out: 0600. She wouldn't miss military time. She looked forward to round-faced, ticking clocks with big hands and little hands.

"I'm ready," she answered.

"You'll be expected at the docking port straight away."

"Tell Oprah Rivera Springer not to get her knickers in a twist, I'll be right there."

"He...she's not going back. Just you and the crew."

Angel shrugged. "I'll be there in a few minutes."

She walked to the porthole one last time, viewing the glistening orb of the Earth. The trip back would take about sixteen hours. They'd land at Kennedy Space Station in Florida and then Air Force One would fly her back to Washington, D.C. That meant in twenty-four hours, roughly, she'd be back in the White House—no, forget that—back in her own private Georgetown townhouse full of ticking clocks, snap shots of old friends, candles and a kitchen with copper-bottom pans and a refrigerator pasted with magnets. Just around the corner, she could get a beer and play a game of pool with a secret service agent at The Paradise Cafe.

Mmm. Twenty-four hours. It was about time.

She made one last check in the mirror. "Don't hate me because I'm beautiful," she said to the smirking reflection. A moment later she exited the drab cubicle that had been her prison among the stars.

The vice president appeared in the hallway, his hair rumpled, dark suit unkempt, tie twisted off to one side, smelling uncharacteristically of cigarettes.

And he was sporting a black eye and a bloody lip.

"Fight?" she asked.

"Political debate."

"Did you win your point?"

He shrugged. "When you're the vice president, you never..." he said taking her bag and moving toward the shuttle with her.

For a moment, his shoulders seemed to collapse, a minor quaking shook his torso, but he collected himself quickly. "Well Angel, dear," he began, downcast, blinking rapidly, his face drawn. The stricken expression he used at state funerals.

Angel gently put an arm around his waist. "Don't, Phil."

"I just wanted to express my regret for..." He removed her hand from his waist and held it in his.

"For what? For having me locked up, wishing we'd never met?"

He stopped, set the bag on the floor, turned, and took her shoulders with both hands, giving her a level stare. "I love you. I really do," he said quietly.

"I know," she said, looking somewhere at his forehead. "I know."

"Do you?"

"Mmm-hmm," she nodded. "I still remember Maui."

"Our honeymoon," he said.

"You promised then that you'd love me until the stars fell out of the sky and the world was no more."

His forehead drew up in a questioning expression.

"That's one promise you kept," she said, twisting out of his grip, stepping backward a step. "Unlike your campaign promises, this one you've kept to the letter."

She turned, bent down and picked up her bag, smiling to herself. Leaving him standing there in the corridor, she walked alone the rest of the way to the shuttle.

♌♌♌

The sky. He could see the sky as if for the first time. Beyond the mountain tops looking like knees and elbows under a dark wool blanket, the wide, star-dusted night sky sheltered the earth. And in the center, the asteroid, larger now, the size of a volleyball.

"Hang on," Concho shouted, staring out ahead into the brilliant white of the headlights.

A moment passed. He knew it was coming. Concho's head made small, jerky searching movements. His eyeballs swiveling in their sockets. Searching the roadway. Searching. Searching.

Then, there it was. A gaping hole.

Whack! The van hit the large, jarring pothole in the road.

What was happening? Concho had known it was coming, had known something was coming in the road ahead.

He leaned forward, resting his weight on the steering wheel. The feeling of illness, of being poisoned by DeBack's venom, had passed. In the feeble light from the instrument panel, he could see that his skin still retained the ruddy, almost orange color. And he still had the sense of flying. Now, though, he was used to it. The venom no longer made him nauseated. It had opened his pores, dilated his eyes, enlarged his blood vessels. His hands felt stronger, more muscular, younger.

And there was something new inside his head, though he couldn't control it and wasn't sure exactly what it was. It seemed like an extra-sensory projection, a beam of invisible light, as though his mind were a winged bat flying invisibly ahead of the van.

More often now, Concho could feel small dangers in the roadway before the van hit them, before they appeared. He could even detect the presence of animals, and a moment later their eyes would glow greenly in the headlights.

What had begun earlier that day as a rushing, plummeting headwind when he had been bitten was now like having mental headlights. A particle beam of thought-senses that swept back and forth like a search light in front and behind. He no longer needed to look in the rearview to see DeBack. He simply knew things.

Like Santa Claus, Concho thought, I can see when DeBack's sleeping and I know when he's awake.

For the moment, DeBack slept, apparently secure in the thought that his bite had turned Concho into some kind of numbed zombie.

Concho, having found several snacks under the seat, burped gaseously and tossed the empty bag of Doritos on the floor along with the six empty beer cans, and an empty donut box. His face was bee-hived in crumbs, his lips greasy and still his stomach growled. He rubbed his bristly chin on the sleeve of his shirt and looked up in time to see the "Welcome to West Virginia" sign that whipped past the van.

Never been so danged hungry. He surveyed the road for a Chevron minimart or an all-night burger stand. Fortunately the end-of-the-world had not yet shut down the fast food industry, although other changes, strange changes, were moving apace.

In the course of the night his feet had grown cramped and swollen inside his boots. He had wanted them off and rather undramatically they had appeared at his side. No puff of smoke. No disappearing, reappearing. Just on his feet one minute, in the passenger's seat the next. All done with concentration, and the energy of DeBack's venom. Think hard enough and it can happen, he thought, smiling.

He sighed happily and for the fourth time that hour he set the cruise control, grasped a bar running across the top of the minivan's windshield and, holding the steering wheel with one hand, he performed a rapid 25 pullups with the other, then reversed the process.

Not even winded.

He felt wonderful. His entire body was glowing, bursting with vigor and his mind felt clear and clean. That venom. DeBack could sell that stuff. Here he'd thought the snake was trying to kill him.

Far from it. That venom was like mother's milk. Dang and double dang—it was better than that. That venom was like a cocktail of anabolic steroids with a chaser of Speed. Also a sensory thought beam.

Yeow-zuh!

His thoughts whisked down spotless marble corridors and moved with the speed and assurance of Olympian muses. That extra-sensory thought-beam still swept back and forth across the roadway. And with each passing moment, Concho was able to understand its signals with greater accuracy, something like fine tuning a radio frequency. When another car was coming around the corner, he pictured it first, then saw it. When a hitchhiker's image flashed through the thought-beam, a grizzled, road-worn figure soon appeared at the side of the highway, thumb extended.

That DeBack, he thought warmly. He works in mysterious ways.

Concho hated to awaken the snake from his slumber, but this venom-induced transformation filled him with such dizzy gratitude he could no longer hold back under the pressure of courtesy.

"Hey, DeBack, snake boy," he whispered, turning to the bench seat where the serpent was fast asleep.

"Hey, fang face, hey." Concho craned around to the back.

"Watch the road," DeBack murmured.

"Hey, I don't need to no more."

"Drive, mortal."

"I don't need to watch the road. You know why?" Concho asked, with a big goofy smile. "Huh? You know why? You wanna know?"

DeBack opened his eyes. Sleepily at first. Then they sprang open and the snake screamed. A wide-mouthed, fangs-extended, eyes-filled-with-terror, girlie-snake scream.

Huh? Concho thought.

Kuh-wham.

The minivan slammed into the back of a parked Wonder Bread truck. And for a long moment there was nothing but silence and darkness and the overpowering scent of enriched white-bread products that build strong bodies twelve ways.

♌♌♌

Through the night time hours they watched. They listened and stared with large eyes over the seat tops as Clifford Clemp, clad in a silver jacket dazzling even under the dim interior lights, stood at the front of the Greyhound bus with an aged, leather-bound Bible in one hand and the driver's mike in the other.

Clemp was like a hipster from the bygone Martini era, smooth talking, head rolling, hair slicked back, eyebrow arching hipster. Reading the irate, prophetic scribble of the Old Testament:

"And I will cast you to the ground," he quoted, his voice pinched and crackling over the bus's overhead intercom. "On the open field I will fling you, and will cause all the birds of the air to settle on you, and I will gorge the beast of the whole earth with you. I will strew your flesh upon the mountains and fill the valleys with your carcass. I will drench the land even to the mountains with your flowing blood. And the watercourses will be full of you. When I blot you out, I will cover the heavens, and make their stars dark. I will cover the sun with a cloud, and the moon shall not give its light. All the bright lights of heaven will I make dark over you, and put darkness upon your land, says the Lord God."

Over the roar of the bus' engine, the conglomeration of ticket-holding riders murmured uneasily to each other. The passenger list included four skinny German students touring the Eastern Seaboard, a housewife who was meeting her sailor husband in New York, a half-dozen glassy-eyed alcoholics wandering the earth, two Puerto Rican strippers with babies, a runaway teenage girl, and two truckers from Des Moines.

One of the truckers, a sun-darkened, deeply wrinkled man in a red cap and a predominately red, plaid, flannel shirt, raised a hand.

"That's from Ezekiel, friends," Clemp said closing his Bible with a sudden snap, then acknowledged the upraised hand. "Yes?"

"Preacher, ain't you got any good things to say?" he asked with a rough-hewn earnest face.

A murmur of agreement trickled through the rest of the bus passengers. The trucker sank back into his seat, but then emboldened by the popular sentiment bubbling all around him, he pressed on. "I mean," the trucker continued, "Ever since Hagerstown it's been gloom and doom. 'I the Lord thy God will smite thee with furious anger' and 'You will be food for worms,' and what have you. Hells Bells, we know the world's going down the toilet. But ain't there some ray of hope somewheres?"

Worried heads nodded up and down the aisle.

Clifford Clemp watched the reaction. A sea of change was sweeping among his Greyhound parishioners, as though the tide of interest was slipping away from him. Lesser men might have backpeddled, but Clemp was seasoned. He had a tension-driven desire to grab them back. The years at Notre Dung proselytizing unsuspecting tourists had infused him with a deep knowledge of how to reel in the human psyche like a kite. He had them where he wanted them. He had been waiting for this moment. Get them stirred up, pry them out of their clam shells, get them on the march, then call the tune. Give the orders.

"Good news?" he chuckled. "You mean with God's bowling ball hurtling toward the earth at this very moment? Now you want the good news? When the hour of destruction is nigh?"

He gripped the mike close to his disapproving mouth, stared down the trucker, then turned his flaming eyes on the others, one-by-one making contact, his sweaty hair falling down into his eyes. They were like curious schoolchildren. Wayward youth. He was the morally outraged father, employer, judge.

The passengers sat motionless, frozen with shame, awaiting their collective sentence. He stared at them. Holding them. Holding them.

"Well," he said in a softer, conceding voice. "There is one slim chance, a possible way out, a big, fat celestial maybe: the narrow road of righteousness. The rocky path begun by many, finished by few. You got to remember, God is a God who sits on the Throne of Justice as well as the Mercy Seat. When he doles out judgment with one hand, he offers the means for grace with the other." His eyelids lowered heavily. "So you may've lucked out."

A *whew* passed over the faces that had moments ago palpitated with terror.

"In Revelation, we read of the New Heaven and the New Earth, for the Old Heaven and the Old Earth have passed away. And this new Kingdom will be inhabited by the *select* who have chosen righteousness. And I cannot over-emphasis the word select. That means few. That means hardly any. One in ten thousand times ten thousand.

The trucker in the red cap began to slowly raise his hand. It crept skyward until Clemp's head swung toward him and javelined him with beady, teed-off eyes.

"So who among you is ready to turn from the Broad Path of Destruction? Who among you is prepared to give up yer evil doings? Yer drinking? Yer drugging? Yer whoring and lying?"

One of the German students raised a hand. "Do you take traveler's checks?"

"What?"

"We're not carrying cash." The other students nodded.

"I'm not in this for money. You can't buy God."

"No, no. To defray your expenses. The expenses of your ministry," shouted a woman from the back, getting out her purse.

The Germans and others nodded and murmured in agreement.

"Oh," Clemp replied. He paused, looked over at the bus driver, then at two or three other nearby faces all turned up to him expectantly. Decision time. He nodded quickly. "Well, that'd be fine. Sure. Sure, okay. Traveler's checks, whatever," he said quietly, dryly.

People throughout the bus reached for bags under seats, stood and wrestled backpacks from overhead compartments. One of the Puerto Rican women looked up from a checkbook and shouted, "How do you spell Clemp?"

The evangelist cleared his throat, shifting the mike from one hand to the other sending out a sparkling ripple from the silver jacket. "Uh, that's C-L-E-M-P. Clemp. Clifford Clemp."

"Look!" a child cried, pressing its excited face to the window.

"Wow," chimed in other voices.

"She's a beauty this time of night," the bus driver said in a gravelly four-pack-a-day voice.

Clemp turned, holding to a chrome safety bar, and ogled the brightly illuminated Statue of Liberty. It stood like a giant white knight in the harbor, preserving immigrants' belief in freedom.

"We're almost to New York?" Clemp asked the driver.

"Yeah, we'll be pulling into the station in another twenty minutes or so."

Clemp felt his heart rate pick up and his mouth tasted suddenly dry. This was his moment. Suddenly chilled, he tugged the silver jacket more tightly around his body. The dream was coming true. He was going to play his part in the unfolding apocalypse. And what would be the result? Would God really destroy His creation? Would He really strew corpses over the face of the earth?

Checks and packets of cash passed hand to hand up the bus aisle. Clemp accepted the bundle wholeheartedly. This was no time to be tainted by mammon, but he had expenses to think about.

He turned back and nodded at his congregation. "Thank you," he said into the mike. "Thanks to each and every one of you. Even servants of the Lord need to pay for hotel rooms."

There was a smattering of applause and a couple Amens.

♌♌♌

The bread truck's driver emerged from a nearby grove of trees zipping up his fly, his mouth hanging agape. When he peered into the wreckage, all the driver could make out was a pile of fast food wrappings, a man slumped over the steering wheel with a snake wrapped around his head.

The following day's paper noted that by all the laws of physics, the wreck should have killed them. "However, anyone who has squashed an entire loaf of Wonder Bread into a fist-sized lump, knows why a snake and a man named Concho survived the crash," a reporter wrote.

Within twenty minutes the scene of the accident in rural West Virginia swarmed with an ambulance, two fire vehicles, several cop cars and a half-dozen sheet metal apprentices from the local Devries Institute.

As if observing from a great distance, Concho felt himself pulled from a solid encasement of Wonder Bread and slammed into the back of the ambulance. Within an hour he was coming back around under the bright lights of an emergency room.

A doctor loomed over the bed, his eyes filled with compassion and wisdom. His youthful, medical face had a quizzical expression, a caring, sensitive look.

"Doc," Concho whispered. "Don't look so worried."

The physician smiled, a beatific, gentle-Jesus smile.

"Please, Doc," Concho murmured, "I'll be okay."

The man in white leaned closer.

"Doc, I'm fine. Really I am. I know you're a skilled and caring professional, but I'm okay."

The physician's forehead wrinkled, an expression of deepening concern, in spite of Concho's assurances, placed a soft, warm hand on Concho's shoulder.

"Do you have health insurance?" the doctor asked, his eyebrows drawing together with tender regards.

"Do I have what?"

"An HMO, perhaps?"

"An H-M-O?" Concho repeated, bewildered at first. Then a sense of recognition dawned on his face. "You questioning my sexuality? 'cause I'm a man's man. I mean—a woman's man. You know. I ain't no H-M-O, I can tell you that much."

"No, no. HMO. Health Maintenance Organization."

"Oh. Like one a them weight-lifting clubs?"

The doctor sighed. "Do you have Blue Cross?"

"Uh, well, let's see, I think I had Yellow Jaundice once and ...Scarlet Fever?"

"Medicaid?"

Concho stared up at the physician and let the word Medicaid drift through his brain, as he shook his head slowly.

"Medicaid?" Concho asked finally. "I don't follow. I am a little thirsty if that's what you mean."

The doctor rolled his eyes and tapped his fingers impatiently on the side of the gurney.

"How do you propose to pay for your health care?"

"What? Ain't you heard. The end of the world is upon us!"

"Not until it's been published in the *New England Journal of Medicine* it ain't. Now, surely you have some method of payment worked out."

"Well don't get mad, doc. Goldang, I just woke up here. I mean it was an accident. I didn't get outa bed this morning and figure my checkbook and think, 'Hey, I got some extra bucks, I think I'll drive into the back of a truck today'. You know? I mean, no offense or nothing."

The doctor made a rapid sucking sound into the back of his teeth, his eyebrows arched, his eyes filled with displeasure, as though calling Concho's bluff.

"I'm serious," Concho said. "I ain't got no money."

"Nothing you can sell?"

"No."

"No time-share condo we could trade out on?"

"No. Honest to God."

"All right then," the doctor groaned. "You can go."

"Really?"

"Yes. I mean it'd be different if you'd had some insurance. I'd have been able to conduct a very expensive MRI, had you hospitalized in the Intensive Care ward and maybe injected a barium solution and put you up on a bi-plane scanner and we would have netted about ten grand, but..." He shrugged as if to say, 'can't win 'em all.'

"I'm okay?"

"You had a nasty snake bite on the back of your neck. That's all."

"Yeah?"

"Fortunately we located the animal and are having it sent down to Atlanta."

"What? Atlanta?" Concho shook his head. "With the end of the world near, you bother sending a snake down to Atlanta?"

"Oh, yeah, standard practice even if the universe is ending. Regulations. Government regulations."

"Where in Atlanta?"

"They'll test him at the Center for Poison Control."

"Test him? How?"

The doctor pulled a finger across his throat. "Probably cut off his head."

"His—wait a minute—his head? No, no, no, no. Listen." Concho grabbed the doctor's white lapels. "You can't do that. That damn rattlesnake means life or death to me. Maybe to the whole human race."

"That was no ratt-ler." The doctor chuckled, extricating himself from Concho's grasp. "And you're damn lucky it didn't mean death."

"Wait. Are we talking about the same snake? About seven feet long?"

"Yes?"

"Big, fat thing with a big old rattle at the end of his tail?"

"Yes, yes, certainly. But hear me out, I'm no expert on the *Sistrus Crotalus*—"

"Sister who?"

"*Sistrus Crotalus,* that's the Latin. As I was saying," he said, "I'm no expert, but I can assure you...that was no rattlesnake. It looked more like..." the doctor paused, reflecting for a moment on the right term.

"More like what?"

"Well. More like a dinosaur, actually. Yes, a legless, wingless dinosaur. I haven't seen the likes of a creature like that since Intro to Paleontology. Gosh that's going back. 1983. Wow, amazing what you retain from the undergrad years."

"A dinosaur..." Concho murmured, thinking back over DeBack's markings. It might make some sense...

"Yes, you know, a dinosaur—big lizard, little brain—Triassic, maybe Mesozoic period. It's hard to say."

"Listen to me, doc..."

"Now that isn't to rule out that this creature may be an ancestor to our modern day rattlesnake."

"Doc..."

"True, this one was larger than the ones you see these days, but still a vertebrate all the same with that horny outer layer of scales. I found his color and his markings most unusual."

"Please just tell me where he..."

"Fascinating creature though. Damned fascinating. Too bad he'll have to be destroyed. Just lie back now, someone will be by to..."

Concho lurched off the gurney. He stood barefoot, wearing only a thin, pale blue hospital gown that gapped wide open in the back.

The physician's mouth popped shut. He stepped back, clutching his clipboard to his chest.

"Listen to me," Concho growled. "You tell me where that friggin' snake is."

His fat finger pounded the doctor's clipboard. It broke in half.

"He's in the animal control van just outside, but..."

Concho took off in a dead run.

"Wait," the doctor shouted after him. "Wait! Leave it to the professionals!"

♌♌♌

Saleem adjusted the telephone and clamped it between his ear and shoulder, freeing a hand so he could tap on the side of the fax machine, then watched expectantly for the lights to blink on. He flipped the on switch back and forth. Nothing. He tapped the plastic casing of the machine with increasing force. Tap, tap. Tap, tap.

"Anything?" Leah asked on the other end of the phone.

"Wait."

Saleem banged twice on the side, then once on the back. The gray LCD bar and two green lights gave a feeble flicker. He clenched his jaw, tightened his fingers into a fist and beat the machine repeatedly until the lights blinked on.

"Okay," he said, slightly winded. "Ready."

"Saleem," Leah said, over the steady crackle of the satellite phone link-up, "I'm giving the phone to Dr. Pitters, all right?"

"Go ahead."

After a pause, Saleem heard a deep voice on the other end. "Pitters here."

"Good morning, sir."

"Your fax working now?" the archeologist asked.

"Looks like it," Saleem replied, training his glare on the row of tiny diode lights with fierce intensity as if to hypnotize the machine into obeying his command.

"Fine. Did Leah give you our location in conjunction with the Dead Sea?"

"Yes," he said, reaching over to a console, pressing a red *receive fax* button. The machine beeped a response and the lights burbled on and off, setting itself with a series of reluctant whirs.

"Okay," Pitters said, "What you need to know is that these are my hand written copies of textual fragments that we found in an unmarked clay pot here at the site. This is all very preliminary. A team of philologists from *Ecole Biblique* is on the way to get an exact translation." Pitters gave a long sigh. "Normally this material would not be released to the public so quickly. In a way it's academic suicide, but under the present circumstances, with the asteroid and the terror that seems to be taking hold around the world, this is an important find."

"There's a connection?"

"So it seems. And by the way, we have not determined as yet the exact order of these fragments, nor have we determined, conclusively, if they are indeed from the same document. My tentative belief is that they *are* from the same document, and I base that on the similarity of the scribal hand."

"Sorry, scribal what?"

"They appear to have been written by the same person. Same scribe, however many thousands of years ago. Same vellum. Same ink."

"Okay."

"All right then, here comes the copies of the two fragments. When they come through, I'll get back on the line to make sure they came over okay."

Almost immediately, Saleem heard the buzz and squeal of the two machines initiating contact, like two exotic insects in a late-night screaming match that will eventually lead to sex. Then plastic wheels inside Saleem's Egyptian-made machine squeaked and squealed, and a curled sheaf of cheap white fax paper began to emerge, line-by-line, from somewhere inside.

FRAGMENT ONE:
The Man and Woman who come out of the ground... who out of one became several, will out of several become one... will save the world from the fiery influence of the serpent... the same shall... righteousness and purity... will walk the second Earth... as a second Adam...

FRAGMENT TWO:
A glittering new star is being... will... to smite the inhabitants of Edam and Persia and Egypt and all the earth... and then a... will rise from the dung of the west... to... the inhabitants of Edam and Persia and Egypt and all the earth... Yet ...will conquer the false star.

When the transmission finished, Saleem tore the sheet free and read it through once. Then held it under the lamp, reading it through a second and third time.

"Saleem," Pitters said, his voice wheedling and warping over the satellite connection.

"Yes."

"How's it look?"

"I don't know what to tell you, sir."

"How's that?"

"There's lots of gaps, lots of dot-dot-dots.

"Any place where you see ellipses and, dots, as you say, is where there are damaged, unreadable portions in the original document."

"Holes?"

"Yes, holes. Deterioration." After a pause, Dr. Pitters continued, "Can you read it back to me?"

Saleem read back the document.

"Sounds good," Pitters said.

"But, what does this have to do with the asteroid?"

"I think when you look at Fragment Two you have to see the parallels—the star and the asteroid. It says, 'a star that rises in the east' is probably the missing part. 'To smite the inhabitants of Edam and Persia and Egypt and all the earth...' To me that sounds like a pretty good description of our own little asteroid."

"But Dr. Pitters, sir, surely you know that ancient writers often wrote in figurative language. And. Well. This sounds almost too literal."

A pause. "You sound like a journalist, Saleem."

"It is my hope to one day be the Sam Donaldson of Palestine."

"Well," Pitters laughed, "You send this fax to the wire services and you'll be on your way."

Saleem smiled and looked over the fax again in a new light, feeling as though he held a map to King Solomon's mines. His head was filled with images of temple scribes and hoary, gesticulating prophets. Heat waves shimmering up in dusty, donkey-dunged streets. And walled cities, limestone pillars, relief carvings of winged lions. Hot wind lifting brightly dyed tapestries of dark warriors. And golden goddesses birthing in the morning sun.

"It speaks of One who will conquer the Star," Saleem said.

"Yes. That's of particular importance, I think."

"This second Adam."

"Right."

"Who is this second Adam?"

"Good question. I think that's where you get into your cherished figurative language. Maybe it's a nuclear missile, who knows."

"Out of several one becomes."

"Or is born from. The text is ambiguous. If we had the entire original document we might be able to determine the meaning. Don't forget, missiles come out of holes in the ground, like the snake in The Garden."

"Couldn't this second Adam be a man?"

"Yes, I suppose, or..." Pitters stopped, then resumed. "Leah reminds me that it could also be a woman."

The phone gave a loud squeal and a series of whining noises.

"Look, Saleem, my batteries are running down here," Pitters shouted on the other end. "Please send this fax on, with the notes I gave you to all the major news networks. I'll be in Jerusalem in two days. We'll set up a news conference."

The phone went dead. Saleem sat staring at the receiver for some time before returning it to its cradle. He walked slowly across the control room, moving past banks of flickering TV screens, absorbed again in the crinkly fax sheet. It felt alive in his hands. The air all about him was heavy with a sense of significance as he remembered his ancestors stretching back over the centuries, back across Roman occupations and Assyrian uprisings and Egyptian captivity. In each time of crisis, a message of hope always arose out of an unnoticed corner. A lowly quarter. A wild man in the desert wearing animal skins shouting poetry. An ass that spoke. A sea that parted. And perhaps, just perhaps this time it was a sheet of paper spun out of a fax machine, a young intern at a television station overlooking Jerusalem. Just perhaps future generations would name a day of deliverance in his honor. A day of feasting for Saleem, the new television personality who gave humanity hope.

♌♌♌

The shuttle dropped out of the clouds over Kennedy Space Center in Florida and gleamed like a diamond in the sky. A minute later the back wheels touched the tarmac, the nose dropped and the vehicle gave a slight shudder. Twin swirls of hot vapor and dust curled behind like ghostly cowabunga waves which were then caught in a blue parachute that emerged from the tail and slowed the craft to a careful, textbook halt.

Small, squat, efficient vehicles buzzed out to the waiting shuttle to receive those inside.

From the shuttle's interior, Angel Williams contemplated her extraordinary fortune at having lived. Even from this vantage point, she could see the death-toting asteroid drawing closer to Earth's blue skies. And yet, emerging from the shuttle, hit with the pure, unrecycled, unfiltered, unspace-station air, she felt a surge of gratitude of having been a mother, to have lived in Washington, to have flown through space, and most of all, to have returned to her beloved terrestrial homeland long enough to enjoy the world's pleasures for a few more days. What luck.

Oh Earth, she thought joyously, you're too wonderful for people to appreciate you.

At the bottom of the stairway she met Colonel Ross in his shining white uniform. He waited for her attentively as she took in the warm breeze and the sun. Then she encountered the Air Force man's intense blue-gray eyes under the polished black rim of his white hat. To have returned to the sight of men like Colonel Ross again...Blessing upon blessing.

"Air Force One is ready, ma'am," he said, with a slight bow.

"What's a girl gotta do to get home?"

"Just click your heels together, ma'am," he replied quietly.

"That's it? Then, I want to start with a cold beer and a game of pool at the Paradise Cafe in D.C."

"And maybe wish upon the nearest star."

The strength left his eyes. Through his blush, Angel could see he regretted that remark. She reached over to touch his cheek.

"Thanks for being so human."

"Not much choice, these days." He shrugged.

"That's exactly why I came back." She circled her hand above her head. "This is the only orbit I want to be in."

She laughed like a sixteen-year-old when he caught her hand, guided her toward the waiting jet. When they reached the stairway, she wondered at the astonished look on the flight attendants' faces. She looked over and realized the source. The Colonel was smiling.

"Why Colonel, you look almost happy."

"Just a funny thought."

"Which is?"

He shook his head.

"Oh, come on."

"Just can't picture you at the Paradise. Pretty rough crowd."

She pretended to be snapping gum, polished her nails against her blouse. "I can hold my own. But I really go there for the food."

"The food?"

"Oh yeah." She snapped her imaginary gum again. "They've got the best ribs in the universe."

♌♌♌

The white and blue Animal Control Van was just emerging from the parking bay outside the emergency room when Concho burst through the doors in his bare feet, his blue robe flapping wildly behind. In a few long, lunging strides, hollering and waving his arms, he reached the side of the vehicle and let out a yell while smashing a fist into the center of the county seal—an Indian warrior seen from the back surveying the mountains, lakes and streams stolen from him—punching a wide dent in the metal skin. The vehicle gave a jolt and slowed just enough to give Concho time to grab the driver's side door handle, rip it open, seize the surprised driver by his belt and shirt collar and yank him out of the van. The county employee rolled over and over like a stunt man in a movie.

Concho hopped behind the wheel of the second stolen van in as many days and sailed out of the parking lot, veering to and fro, until he bounced over a curb and hit the street with a loud scraping sound. He squealed off in hot pursuit of the world's salvation, calling over his shoulder, "Hey DeBack."

No reply.

"Hey, DeBack," Concho yelled again, his body pumping with adrenaline.

He glanced backward long enough to see a large burlap sack wrestling with itself in the large space at the rear of the van.

Concho laughed and said, "Don't worry, I'll get you outta there."

He surveyed the scene out the front and side windows. They were in a small burg in Appalachia. A hardware store, video store, bait shop, a scattering of tattered two story houses. A tiny human collection where the men mined coal and the women dreamed of becoming another Patsy Cline.

Concho wheeled the van around behind an abandoned furniture store with graffiti scrawled in the large white-soaped windows. He wheeled this way and that, through deep, beat-out ruts and finally came to a stop. When he cut the engine he could hear the serpent grunting and cursing in the back.

"Hey," he laughed, "What'll you give me if I get you outta there?"

"Kckinthfcs."

"Huh?" Concho called out, vastly amused with himself. "Can't quite make that out."

He reached down and loosened the mouth of the bag and out flew DeBack, angry and panting. The snake searched the walls wild-eyed, roving around in the back of the van, his narrow, serpent chest heaving.

"I'll give you a kick in the fathe, that'th what," DeBack sputtered.

"Kick in the face," Concho repeated. "Well that's pretty ballsy, coming from a guy who don't have no arms or legs."

"Well if you..." DeBack froze in mid-retort. His beady eyes bunged out of his triangular skull.

"You okay?" Concho chuckled.

DeBack eyed Concho with sudden suspicion. "You're thure kicking around like a thpring chicken."

"I feel great!" Concho said, enthused. "I have to admit when yuh first bit me I was a little ticked off. But now I feel better than ever."

"Better than ever," DeBack murmured.

"What the hell's in that stuff?"

DeBack slid away from the bag and brought his huge snake face right up into Concho's, gazing into the man's clear, bright eyes with a kind of medical intensity, as though examining Concho in the same way as the physician back in the ER.

"I'll tell you what'th in that thtuff... probably thome of the oldest DNA on the planet," DeBack said.

"Well whatever! It suits me just fine."

"Doeth it?" the serpent hissed.

"Feels like I just had a valve job. Like my brain's been roto-rootered."

"Well there'th more where that came from, but for now we have to go."

"Oh, right! Where to?"

"Heaven'th Gate, remember?"

"Right, we need that last apple."

"Exactly."

"Why?"

"Why what?"

"Why do we need the last apple?"

"You'll thee."

"I will?"

DeBack nodded, his eyes piercing an invisible spot on the windshield.

"You know how to get there?"

"Oh..." DeBack said in a velvety voice. "I could get there with my eyeth clothed."

The serpent broke his stare and wound his way up to the front of the van and curled up in the sunny passenger's seat.

Concho hunched to the front and settled behind the wheel and started up the engine. He revved the engine a couple of times and then looked over at DeBack.

"You're not really a rattlesnake, are you?"

"Heaven'th," DeBack replied. "What made you think I was a rattlethnake?"

Concho put the van in gear and carefully pulled out from behind the abandoned store.

"I guess, the rattle?"

"Thith?" the snake asked, lifting the tan-colored, multi-ridged rattle at the tip of his tail, giving it a good shake. "Purely show buthinethth, I athure you."

"Really."

"Oh, yeth," he said with a chuckle.

"Wow, 'cause the doctor back at that hospital had you pegged for a dinosaur."

"A dinothaur," DeBack replied with a hint of wounded pride. "I was around long before the dinothaurth."

Concho wheeled the vehicle back onto the main road and quickly out of town. The roadway on both sides was lined with thick trees and jagged, towering mountains.

"Guess I'm not much of a reptile expert," Concho said.

DeBack sounded demure. "Well... if I were to be entirely honetht, I guess I have to take partial rethponthibility for the dinothaurth."

"You what?"

DeBack avoided Concho's amazed glances. "Yeth, well, the Earth wath no longer new. Original Thin was established...I wath banithhed to an athtonithhingly barren region of Methopotamia."

"Yeah?" Concho asked, anticipating the gist of the tale.

"I ran into a thhe-hippo and... looking back I thuppothe it wath the challenge of it."

"Of what?"

"Of it. IT."

"You boinked a hippo?"

"You have a way of making beautiful thingth thound tho crude."

"You boinked a hippo!" Concho brayed.

"Thhe was willing and over twenty-one..."

"Yeah, over twenty-one hundred pounds."

"And I wath... young."

"You," Concho shook his head. "Wait. I'm just trying to work out the...the physics of the maneuver. You made the camel with a hippo."

DeBack sighed. "Yeth."

"How?"

"I wath bored."

"Okay. You were bored. But that's not the question. The questions is *how*?"

DeBack's mouth twisted to one side and his head rose up several inches as if engaged in watching the road.

"It involved..." he began, then his tone changed. "Look, thith is adolethcent."

"No really, I'd like to know. We have time."

DeBack paused, then explained, "Let me just thay, it involved an incline, thome vineth and a fair amount of thkill."

"Skill."

"Yeth."

"Vines. That's it. Vines."

"And the female was extremely willing," he said quickly, and then added with the bored voice of a sophisticate, "Ath I thaid, it wath Methopotamia. There wathn't much else going on."

"And so from this little one night stand..."

"The rethulting offthpring looked like the Loch Neth Monthter."

"You must have been so proud."

"Funny," his eyes lidded in languorous memory. "Actually, I wath proud, until God found out."

"What'd he do?"

"Thee any dinothaurth around, lately?"

"No."

"It wathn't pretty."

The van came to a four-way stop.

"Which way, Big Daddy?"

"North. We thould get there in about half an hour."

♌♌♌

From inside the silver jacket, Clifford Clemp withdrew a small address book decorated on the cover with an illustration of Jesus in boxing gloves with the words, "Lean, Mean, Redemption Machine."

He flipped past numerous pages of telephone numbers and postal addresses of tourists he had converted over the years at Notre Dung. Citizens of New York were notoriously the most difficult to win over to Christ, but once they'd turned from their sinful ways they became the most violently righteous soul-winners one could ever hope to meet.

Norm Zwetlot had been one such case. The man used to drink Scotch whisky to wash down his breakfast eggs and wound up each night at an S&M bar with electrodes attached to his testicles. Once the light of the Gospel had shone through the murk and mist of his unholiness, he'd given up all that in addition to profanity, spousal abuse and unsafe driving practices.

A former maitre d', Zwetlot now preferred waiting tables because it gave him more time with people. His specialty had been saying grace for the diners, whether they wanted it or not.

Clemp flipped all the way to the end of the book and found the number for Zwetlot. For a second he savored the unusual success of winning this wandering NYC lamb to the Lord, then he scraped some dog doo off his shoe and dropped a coin into the telephone and typed in the number. As the phone began to ring, Clemp looked all around him. Here he was at last, another step closer to the dream of standing in the middle of New York City wearing the silver jacket, poised to take the celebrity world by storm with his message of hope for sinners. None of that cheap grace mind you, no sir. A person had to earn a spot in Heaven. And it took sweat and tears and prayers. After all, even the Gem of Great Price was only found after plowing up an entire Arkansas field, but it could be done if only...

"Hello, Jesus loves you."

"Jesus loves you back. Hello, Norm?" Clemp inquired.

"Clemp? Is that you? Clifford Clemp? How the health, education and welfare are you?"

"Hi, Norm, doing fine. Doing fine."

"How's things at Our Lady of Perpetual Droppings?"

"Well that's what I'm calling about. I'm not at Notre Dung."

"No shift? Whatcha up to?"

"Listen, Norm. You sitting down?" Clemp laughed. "I'm in New York."

"What? Nuevo Yorko?"

"Yes. I'm here to preach the message. I'm wearing my silver jacket."

A loud whooping sound came from the other end. "Just in time. Just in time. Have you read the news?"

"Yeah, but it's more than that."

"Have you read the papers today?"

"No. Been on the bus all day."

"Where you at?"

"I'm standing here directly in front of Grand Central Station."

"I'll be right down. But before I get there, brother, go buy a paper."

"Newsstands are open this time of night?"

"Yeah. Go right now. There's an all-night newsstand inside the station. I'll be there in twenty."

"Okay. Which one? Which paper?"

"Don't matter. Just buy a paper and read the headlines."

"Okay."

The phone on the other end clicked and went dead. Clemp exited the phone booth and walked back inside the station to the newsstand. Most of the daily papers had been purchased. There were three left. A New York Times, a Houston Post, and a Chicago Tribune. What he saw made his heart pump faster. In huge type the *New York Times* read, "ASTEROID AVENGER!"

The Houston paper read, "DEAD SEA SCROLL PREDICTS 2nd ADAM KICKS ASTERIOD'S BUTT!"

A third paper, the *Chicago Tribune* read, "ADAM TWO, WHERE ARE YOU?"

Clemp picked up this last paper, paid the vendor, walked outside to a nearby, brightly lit window, and read through the article describing the find near the Dead Sea. Two tiny scroll fragments appeared to offer some hope for the impending apocalypse. In a sidebar to the article, Jesse Jackson was quoted as saying that he too had received such a message from a 900-foot Oral Roberts in a strange dream only the night before.

Clemp looked up into the late night sky and between the towers of New York, he could see the asteroid larger and brighter now than ever before. Even though it was still thousands of miles from the outer reaches of earth's atmosphere, it was about the size of a tiny round autumn moon.

The sky had taken on a dull, golden haze and the very air seemed to press down onto the sidewalk.

Looking up from the paper he took in the street nearby. Cars and busses, bumper to bumper, people crushing together in a desperate attempt to escape the city. A noise of ecstasy caught his attention. Two men in a stalled car, parked halfway on the sidewalk, cried out in pleasure as their lean, nude bodies pounded together in a microscopic Hyundai back seat. Teenagers without a stitch on raced through the night, between packed cars, their young lithe bodies dancing as they smashed windows, pelted buildings with eggs, urinated from the tops of trucks. Hunched men and women, wearing their finest Banana Republic attire, were quietly shooting heroin.

Even with the unchecked chaos, a strange, strangled quiet, a superstitious oppression hung over the city. Only the sound of an occasional splintering window broke the stillness that hovered around Clemp.

He leaned heavily against a building, panting for breath. The dream had not played out like this. In the dream, world conditions were at their normal pace. There had not been these high stakes. Where did he fit in?

He was just one man from Texas. For years his mother had spoken in a rushed whisper about the vision of Clemp standing in the world-famous Rainbow Room, wearing the jacket, unleashing his furious, bound-for-hell message to a crowd of hip unbelievers. The most influential artists and investors of the age.

The vision of a mother who wished her son to be a part of that globe-trotting crowd. The Liza Minnelli Crowd. The David Geffen Crowd. The Liz Taylor Crowd. The Peter Jennings Crowd. The Lawrence Tish Crowd. The people who lived between the pages of *People* and *The Wall Street Journal*.

Looking around at the nightmare surrounding him, Clemp had to ask himself if those beautiful people really existed? Would they appear when the morning dawned? Without the limousines and the film premiers? The paparazzi? The diamond-studded sunglasses and designer underwear? Without them this collection of streets and skyscrapers might just as well be Cleveland.

For a moment he removed the jacket, holding it before his eyes so that it caught glints off the lights of a doomed city and a yellowish sky. Would he really make a difference? Would he be the one to get these *gens du monde* straight?

Or would this Second Adam make an appearance at the planet's last moment and denude the dream before he even got his start?

Suddenly Clemp's resolve, his thrill, his V-rocket trajectory seemed to cascade about him. This city of New York that had existed like the Home of the Gods all those years in all those glossy magazines now appeared to him like some weird, wasted, trashy, blind-reptile level of Dante's Inferno. Had he reached the Emerald City, only to discover that the Wizard was just a figment of Frank L. Baum's, let's-sell-a-series-of-children's-books, imagination?

No. No.

He, Clifford Clemp, would not be relegated to history's nosebleed section like some modern day John the Baptist. He would not roll out the red carpet so some Savior-Come-Lately could clean up on the interviews and movie rights.

If the world wanted a Second Adam, if America's gnawing publicity-starved gullet craved a Messiah, then by God and by Satan and by Cracky they would get one. His name would be...

"Clifford Clemp!" shouted a familiar voice.

Clemp wheeled around.

"Norm!"

Norm Zwetlot ambled up the sidewalk in chinos and an expensive dark silk shirt. His black, thinning hair combed back over a wide, smooth head. He smiled broadly, pushing back two large dimples toward his big, pink ears.

Clemp slapped the shining jacket back on with a loud snap and gave Zwetlot a showy, back-slapping hug.

"What the health brings you to Gotham?" Zwetlot asked.

Clemp held up the newspaper, folded so that the word Adam showed.

"God called me here," he said. "Called me in a dream. For such a time as this I came into the world."

Zwetlot looked from Clemp in the silver jacket to the headlines. His eyes blinked rapidly as though recovering from a fainting spell. He swallowed and smacked his forehead with the palm of his hand.

"It's you, isn't it. It's you!"

Clemp nodded, a mute smile blossoming on his face. He pointed to the newsprint, "...will rise from the dung of the West."

"You're the Second Adam?" Zwetlot looked faint for a moment, then clapped Clemp on the shoulder. "You are the Second Adam!"

The men and women shooting heroin looked up from their needles. The two men in the back of the Hyundai craned their heads out of the open back window. A young teenage girl, her naked chest smeared in blue paint, peered out from behind a taxi cab.

"I want to treat you to dinner tomorrow evening, where I work," Zwetlot said. "Are you up to that?"

"Wonderful, but not necessary."

Zwetlot did an "aw shucks" motion, and grinned. "You'll like it. Very New York. A must for every visitor."

"Great. Where, what time?"

"Eight o'clock, tomorrow night..." Zwetlot gave Clemp his biggest smile yet. "...at the Rainbow Room."

♌♌♌

Heaven's Gate looked like a three-mile-wide, milk-white breast. Nestled among low, rambling Virginia hills, the huge circular Christian amusement park was the largest enclosed family attraction in the world. Something like 1,280 acres was under one domed roof that sloped upward to an observatory at the center. An 800-foot, Chinese-made mirror with a myriad of lenses was trained on the point in the sky where, according to Reverend Raymond Friend, the actual City of God lay just beyond the gloriously yawning mouth of the Orion Nebula. Those who watched the brightly orange nebula cloud night after night claimed to have seen angels dancing like fireflies about the entrance, guarding Heaven from elements of a universe in decline.

Concho steered the van down and out of the Appalachian mountains and approached the short-term parking area of Heaven's Gate.

"You got some sort of plan here?" Concho asked, driving through a vehicle entrance, reaching out the window, pressing a large green button and taking the ticket that fed out.

"The firtht need ith clotheth."

Concho looked down at his skimpy hospital gown, stretched across his legs like a miniskirt. "Yeah, we'll need 'em for both of us, once we get the apple. Can't have you wandering around inside there buck naked and me dressed in this here muumuu."

"You're fine. I'm the one who needth thomething."

"I'm not fine." Concho pulled the van into an empty space. "Look at me."

"All you need ith thome kind of belt or thhathh," DeBack said.

"What... a sash?"

"You're going in, in character. You're going ath a Biblical character. You know, like at a Renaiththance Fair."

"Oh. They do that here?"

"Look outthide."

Passing close by was a tall, reedy man with short, parted-on-the-side accountant hair and steel-rimmed glasses while wearing a long, striped, flowing robe and crude leather sandals. He wore a long white false beard and held in one hand a smooth-polished, gnarled walking stick. Behind followed his wife and two daughters all wearing thick glasses, all dressed exactly alike except for the beards.

"So it's a big costume party?" Concho said.

"Well, not exactly a party per thay. Remember what I thaid about Puritanth and partieth."

"Oh, are these Puritans too?"

"Of a different thtripe, yeth."

Concho opened the door and eased out. A couple cars down he spied a large camper that appeared to be empty.

"DeBack, there's some curtains in the windows of that camper over there. Might make me a good sash."

"Yeth, but hurry up, then!"

Concho looked all around in the parking area. Seeing his moment, he walked to the back of the camper and knocked loudly on the door. "Hello? Hello in there?"

He waited for a response. No response.

Concho grabbed the door handle in both hammy hands and grimaced and twisted the knob slowly out of the aluminum door to the sounds of metal sheering and snapping. When the knob was pulled free, he tossed it under the camper. With the door wide open, he grabbed both sides of the door frame and launched himself inside. The quarters were cramped, not an inch of space wasted. Little cabinets and lockers tucked away, tables that pulled out of the walls, seats that were housed in nooks and crannies. The whole place stank of hot dogs. In one quick jerk he snapped the curtains out of the window. The fabric was a rough bumpy material the color of French's Mustard. He tore them into strips, tied the strips together and then tied the whole thing around his waist effectively shutting the gown in back while simultaneously giving him the look of an extra in a Cecil B. DeMille Roman epic.

With that finished, he felt another stab of hunger and opened the small refrigerator to find it filled with cold cuts, Cheese Whiz, hotdogs, relish, catsup and beer. Ravenously he consumed handfuls of meat and condiments. Stuffing his mouth leaking catsup out the corners of his lips. He chug-a-lugged can after can of foamy Keystone beer.

As he stood, preparing to go, his eye fell on a copy of Newsweek, laying near the stove. The cover photo was a take of an ancient fragment of writing in Hebrew, overlaid with the headline, *Asteroid Relief.* A subhead went:

A small remnant of 3,000 year old sheep skin holds message of redemption for a world in its last hour.

Adam Two — Where are you?

Concho flipped past the first couple of pages. Adam Two? What was all this about? In the center spread, he read the translated texts found by prominent archeologist Dr. Pitters and his team near the Dead Sea, and then skimmed the analysis of how the text might or might not apply to the current asteroid situation.

In a sidebar he saw a photo of a man he recognized vaguely at first, then with a grin of recognition. In a small article titled, *Will the Real Second Adam Please Stand Up,* he saw Clifford Clemp, the guy he and DeBack had scammed the biplane from. Clemp had gotten to New York wearing that ridiculous silver jacket DeBack had given him and was now going around telling people that he was the second Adam and that he was going to bust the asteroid's chops. In all parts of the world, the article went on to say, loudmouths and wisecrackers were declaring themselves to be Adam reborn and amassing followings where they might.

"Fool's names and fools faces always appear in public places," Concho grumbled. Flipping at random through the magazine now, seeing all the thousands of words, seeing all the faces flash past, seeing...

Seeing...

Seeing...

Seeing... her.

His hands began to tremble so badly the magazine slipped and slapped onto the floor.

Her.

He knelt and fumbled madly around the grease-stained linoleum, grappling against his own frazzled nervous system. With weak, shaky hands he managed to get the magazine up on a low table and he lay on the floor for a minute getting his breath, swallowing back the bitter-sweet lump in his throat.

He closed his eyes, breathing hard—images firing away in his brain. Green broad leaves, moss-encrusted rocks, vines swinging all about, a rich, humid place of promise. And Her. He'd been running from that wrecking-ball voice behind him, trying to find her.

The lovely dark-eyed woman with thick, ringlets of black hair, surrounded by falling rose petals.

He had been looking for his lover, his companion. Her.

His innocent bride.

He had been looking for the woman who may as well have been formed from the stuff of his own body, the way he loved her. His other self in a wild and violent universe.

Slowly the wave of thick anxiety and sobering shock began to subside and he was able to sit up and take the magazine with both hands. In the gossip section was a small headline, *Angel Williams Takes Flight,* with a short piece on the wife of the vice president, who had chosen to spend her last days on earth, rather than in the safe confines of the space station.

"This is my home, not some metal rat trap in the sky," the article quoted her as saying. "The minute I get my sea legs back, I'm heading over to the Paradise Cafe in D.C. and get rid of them. Six apple daiquiris should just about do the trick." A small photo showed her smiling radiantly.

It was her. Concho stared at the photo that accompanied the article. No telling where his memory had gone, or what strange dimension his real self was trapped in. This woman was his lover and companion. A beacon began flashing somewhere inside him where once there had been a calcified, ancient yearning place. It was warming now, coming to life. She was the one he had been looking for. The one he had been running to in the dream. Or was it a dream?

Dreams and memories look a lot alike on the old mental drive-in movie screen.

Memories. That green on the bottoms of his feet in the not jail cell. That hadn't been a dream. More like a vision. A belch of pregeologic remembrance. An hallucination. A sign, perhaps.

Slowly he stood up and peered out the curtainless window of the camper. He could see DeBack's head swaying, motioning for him to return pronto. Mouthing words of urgency.

Concho sank back on his haunches. The strange events surrounding him suddenly began to make sense. Worrisome thoughts converged like skydivers on some internal landing pad.Complete global destruction was less than twenty-four hours away. Yet all he cared about now was that this Angel Williams—married or not, she was his angel—was in Washington, D.C.

The ancient serpent, DeBack was headed for Washington, D.C. and dragging Concho/Adam along with him. Concho shook his head. Hallucinations. He was as bad as that lunatic Clemp. Adam, Eve and the Snake.

As if God would let the same three stooges, who had screwed up the world in the first place, get together for a second go around. Concho shook his head trying to dislodge the confusion wedged there like a stone in a pipe. Getting together again like some diabolic, cosmic alumni reunion. But for what purpose? To save the world from a celestial croquet ball?

Or was this some form of perverse revenge, allowing Angel and Concho to see the results of their original transgression?

He was surely hallucinating. This whole thing was one long LSD voyage. He would come crashing down from the high and discover he was some pip-squeak junior in college, trying to understand Jung with every turn of the page.

"Yeah, sure," he muttered. "You're Adam Two, all right, Concho old boy. And the Pope is Canadian."

But he couldn't shake the eerie feeling. If it was all true, then DeBack had to know Angel was Eve. And he was or had been Adam. His mind went back to the earlier, on-the-road conversation when he had pressed DeBack for a clearer picture of the afterlife and about the mechanics of reincarnation. The snake had pretended no real clue, had just said, "How should I know, I've never died."

Concho stood again and made an effort to clear his mind. If his own newly-enhanced thought-beam could pick things up—then DeBack's must be a hundred times stronger. He glanced back toward the van again. Somehow he would have to go back to being the dumb cowpoke he'd been only a few days before. At least until he figured all this out.

He tore out the page, folded it into his sash, rummaged through the closet for some clothes for DeBack, then hopped out the back of the camper and made his way to the van.

"What took you tho long?" DeBack demanded.

"Well, dang it, I got the hungries again. They had a whole 'frigerator load of hotdogs and stuff."

DeBack stared at him for an uncomfortable time. "And?"

Concho blushed. "And a girlie magazine."

DeBack grunted unhappily. "We don't have time for any of that! Don't see any thandalth."

"I know, I know. Don't have time for girlie magazines. The shoes all looked too small for your soon-to-be-again gnarled feet."

Concho whirled around and around and asked, "Say how do I look in this outfit?"

"Like a Roman gigolo."

"Good, that's the effect I was aimin' for."

♌♌♌

Panic rolled over lazily. When his hand didn't encounter the body he expected to find, he swept the entire area of the sheet, then reached over and clicked on the light.

Oprah Rivera Springer stood looking out the observation window, wearing the outfit of an old-fashioned aviator: goggles, leather jacket, jodhpurs.

"Come back to bed," Panic motioned. "As your Commander-in-Chief I..."

A shake of his/her head. "No time."

"True," Panic let his head fall onto the pillow, reached for a cigarette, "but I thought we'd sort of go out with a bang."

Oprah Rivera Springer smiled, a sunburst of white teeth beneath the mustache. "Didn't you hear? Someone on the intercom telling us about the *find* near the ..."

"Yeah, so what?"

"The Man and Woman who come out of the ground... who out of one became several, will out of several become one..."

"You think...you're the Second...?"

"Adam." She smiled. "I don't think. I know."

Panic closed his eyes. "What are you going to do?"

"Not just me, *we* are going to stop the asteroid."

The president's eyes opened wide.

She/he grinned. "Just think of yourself as Teddy Roosevelt charging up San Juan Hill." She knelt beside the bed. "We can still go out with a bang, Mr. President."

Panic groaned as she opened his pajama bottoms.

"And just think of the ratings."

♌♌♌

The midway at Heaven's Gate was filled with resolute Christians, all marching and praying, singing and holding hands, their eyes glazed. This was the moment, the test they'd all been waiting for. The ultimate pass/fail.

And each paid forty-nine dollars and forty-nine cents.

"Kinda awe-inspiring, don't you think?" Concho whispered to the bag he carried over his shoulder that held DeBack and his clothes.

"They had lotth of practice," DeBack lisped back. "Protethting at all those abortion clinicth."

Concho's smile glazed over when several nearby worshipers noticed him talking to the leather bag. He put both hands over his heart and looked to heaven. They followed suit and he slipped away, knifing through the stream of humanity to the opposite bank.

The flow carried Concho past the Crown of Thorns roller coaster, which was purported to move so fast that blood appeared on the foreheads of the truly saved, while other excretions arrived for those just scared as hell. Concho tried to see the faces of the riders. He watched for the same look as those on the midway. But the cars swooped by too fast to see them. No one was waving their arms or screaming.

The stoic multitude waiting in line to see the John The Baptist Pavilion stretched several blocks. Couples lined up to take their last picture. Men stuck their heads through a hole in a platter that Salome held while the photographer said, "Cheese."

The Lion's Den was similarly enjoyed by the Protestants. The Biblical counterpart to a Halloween maze. Devotees walked through a dark corridor as lions' paws reached out or a flame flared up in front of them. Not for the faint of heart, according to the entrance sign.

Just past an encyclopedic petting zoo was an exhibit called The Flood which made Concho's hands and fingers shake, so much so that he had to fight to keep hold of DeBack in his leather tobacco-pouch-bag. A group of ten people (two-by-two) boarded their own personal Ark to ride out the ancient liquid holocaust, while drowning animals and sinners rose out of the boiling waters at appropriate intervals to clutch at the sides of the metal-made-to-look-like-wood Ark.

The whole scene was Hollywood and Gomorrah.

"I don't get it, DeBack," Concho whispered into the sack, "Why are all these people here?"

"Look at one of the ticketth."

Concho searched the ground until he found one. He read through the conditions, the price, and finally came to the disclosure: 'Only those patrons actually in attendance the moment the earth is destroyed, will be guaranteed salvation.'

He looked up. The sky was filled with a shimmering black ghost of the rock taking a bead on the Earth.

♌♌♌

"Now, that's what I call a de-briefing," Angel said, then leaned back and sighed.

Colonel Ross blushed.

She stroked his arm. "If I had known you were in charge of Air Force One, I would have made Phil run for President seven years ago."

He stretched toward her, whispered, "If I had known about you, I would have assassinated him six years ago."

She curled her arm around him, pulled him closer. How could she tell him that every man she'd ever met had fallen in love with her—except her husband.

"Still want to go to the Paradise?"

She smiled, kissed his forehead. "Later," she said, curling her long slim legs around him tightly.

♌♌♌

The right Reverend Raymond Friend looked like Harry Truman with Jimmy Carter's teeth. He was one of nature's oddities. Devoid of beauty, he was trusted by one and all, immediately on sight.

Concho stood looking up at the seventy-by-seventy foot screen that carried the man's assuming features. The biggest crowd yet swarmed the square around the video cathedral.

"Where's the apple?" he whispered to DeBack.

"Do you thee a tall, glath croth?"

"A glass cross..." Concho looked. "Yeah, over to our left. Huge sucker."

"It'th in the upper eatht wing. All you have to do ith thneak in and grab it."

Concho looked at the building and the crowd. Spotted the guards with submachine guns at what looked to be every level.

"Hell, the greateth police forceth in the country couldn't keep thith theft from happening."

"I'm not so sure," Concho replied.

"Why?"

"It's a glass building, surrounded by guys with really big guns, and at least a half-million people watching."

"Piethe of cake."

"Yeah, right."

"Actually," DeBack's eyes were bright, "it'th a piethe of gum. Reach in here, take thith piethe of gum and chew."

Concho reached into the leather bag, pulled out the gum, held it at arms length. He eyed it suspiciously. "You want me to put this in my mouth?"

"Yeth. Then take off your clotheth, quick."

Concho twisted his head and looked inside at the snake.

"They won't be able to thee you," DeBack chided. "The gum will make you invithible to the human eye."

"What about dogs?"

He laughed, "You'll still thmell, I thuppothe.

"Put me down by the talletht tree near the croth, I'll make my way into the highetht brancheth."

Concho laid the bag on the ground, and hoped against hope that DeBack wouldn't get stepped on. He stripped off his clothes, chewed down on the gum and quickly pushed himself through the people like the prow of a ship pushes through ocean waves.

Mortification, pure and simple. But he kept his shame at bay by keeping a strict count on the number of times he chewed, climbing the stairs to the entrance of the cross. The gum would last as long as the flavor held out. One chew every forty-eight seconds would prolong the flavor for about twenty-five minutes.

The guards searched the crowd, religiously. Beady eyes scanning right to left, up and down. Not once did they focus on Concho as he approached.

Unfortunately, the doors were closed. He chewed once stopped. There wasn't time to wait for someone to show up. He looked at the nearest guard, made a buzzing sound, then pinched the skin on the back of the man's neck.

"Ow! Lord that hurt."

The other guards came to his aid. "Bee?"

"Felt more like a wasp."

"Devil take them. Better go in and have it looked at."

The wounded guard nodded, stepped on the pad. The doors whooshed open and Concho whooshed in with the guard.

Next hurdle was steps or elevator? The sign said the museum of artifacts was on the seventh floor. Concho opted for the steps.

Midway between the third and fourth floor, he encountered a man and a woman walking hand-in-hand. No way past them. He followed them up another flight of stairs. Listening to their cooing debate.

"But, Darling," she said. "If we get married just so we can... you know. Won't that hurt our chances in heaven?" A finger twirled in her peroxide blond hair. "After all, the purpose of sex is to reproduce, and we know there's not enough time to make a baby."

The man's eyes rolled, but he obviously held back his first choice of comments.

"I know, Snookums, but I just want to be married to you when the world ends. I don't care about the other."

She looked at him, melted. "I'm yours, Clement."

"And I'm yours, Clementine," he replied.

As they embraced, Concho slipped past, grateful they didn't have time to make a baby with names like that.

"Oh, my gosh." Clementine gasped.

"What is it?"

"I thought I felt something brush by us, then up there..."

Concho had forgotten to chew. He ground his teeth twice on the gum and slipped around the corner of the stairway.

"I don't see anything," Clement said. "Maybe it was an angel blessing our decision."

"Oh, Clement."

"Oh, Clementine."

Concho struggled with the pain when he accidentally bit the inside of his mouth.

On the seventh floor, Concho followed the sign to the east wing. He sensed the red trip alarm beam on the display case before ever seeing it. He took a moment to look out the window. DeBack had said he would be in the top branches. If anything went wrong, he was to smash the glass window and throw the apple to that tree. DeBack would do the rest.

Concho chewed down on the gum. Awful stuff. Cinnamon wasn't his favorite flavor.

He gazed at the apple. Yep, just like the others—pruny as pruny can be.

He stared at the glass display case. Looked out the window toward the tree again. Looked for DeBack. Knew there was no way everything would go as planned.

Out across the horizon, Concho saw a helicopter approaching. Above it was the asteroid. Reverend Raymond Friend's face glistened, seventy feet up in the air.

"Aw, shit," Concho moaned, then pounded his fist through the glass box that held the apple. "Goldanged snake, anyway."

A siren screamed. All eyes from below turned upward. Footsteps echoed throughout the glass building.

Concho chewed, grabbed a desk chair and threw it through the window facing the tree. He grabbed the pruny apple, gave it a mighty heave toward the crown of leaves.

"You better be in there, you slimy reptile," he said, turning to face a crowd of angry, alarmed Christians.

"Damn, I'm really getting tired of you guys with guns."

"Hey, you. Pervert. Put your hands up," called a woman guard.

Concho chewed twice, three times. No juice or flavor, the gum was disintegrating. He hunkered down, squatting, hands around his knees.

"Stand and put your hands up," she repeated.

Concho shrugged. "Your choice," he said standing, raising his hands over his head.

"Jesus Christ. Sit," she said slowly.

"Put your hands down. Here, cover yourself," she yelled, pitching him her jacket.

"Have you no shame?" came another voice.

The crowd gasped. Concho stared into the very real eyes of Reverend Raymond Friend.

God's favorite angel.

♌♌♌

Clifford Clemp sat in the kitchen, trying to keep the flying sauces and drips of meat from hitting his jacket. Zwetlot had been true to his word. Not only was Clemp going to have the finest dinner in his life, but Zwetlot had gotten a look at the night's entertainment.

"You go up there, see? Right after Bill Haley, III. There's suppose to be a comedian, but I'll have the bartender slip him a mickey. No one will know the difference until it's too late."

Clemp mulled a sermon over in his mind. He felt not a whit of fear or uneasiness. It was as if all those years preaching to one or two, or none at Notre Dung had prepared him for New York.

He gazed out the window at the smog-ridden spires and antsy humanity below.

If anyone had been properly prepared for New York, it was Clifford Clemp, a.k.a. Adam Two. He grabbed a tall-stemmed glass from a waiter and gulped down the contents, coughing, nearly gagging as the olive caught where his tonsils use to be.

"Bring me a couple more of these," he wheezed. Then, to the cigarette girl on her break, "I'm gonna preach in the Rainbow Room, jus' like my mama dreamt."

"That's nice. Want a box of chocolates?"

"What for?"

"Why not? They say life is like a box of chocolates. Don't you like chocolates?"

Clifford shook his head adamantly. "My mama says life is hard and if you ain't got religion when you're done, you're cooked."

The cigarette girl shuddered. "Oooh. That's awful."

He grabbed her by the hand and dragged her to a window, pointing to the approaching asteroid, which filled the sky like the moon in chiffon drag.

"That's awful! That's the awful truth." he smiled, loopy. "But you're gonna get some 'ligion tonight, darlin'. Just you wait and see."

Concho blinked twice, ready to duck if the enraged Reverend Raymond Friend should decide to take the punch he'd had balled up in his fists for fifteen minutes. Concho had told him everything, the truth, the whole truth, and nothing but the truth.

Waking up in the desert. The talking serpent. The Cave. The Bag of Tricks and its contents. The silver jacket, the spark plug, the cinnamon gum. Everything.

Friend listened and paced the length of his office, staring grimly out across the expanse of the theme park. A small ferret-like animal, an exotic pet, rode on the man's shoulders cooing and chattering as if imitating Concho's voice.

Friend reached up, removed the animal and stretched it out on the desk, rubbing its neck between powerful fingers. He couldn't stop shaking his head.

"If it wasn't so tragic, I'd laugh. I mean..." he began pacing the room again, "... for forty years I develop a ministry, this whole theme park, satellite programming, video tape series...Everything I could possibly do to attract that low-down, good-for-nothing snake, and you sneak in, break a window, and throw him that goddamned pruny thing with a million people watching."

Concho had the terrible urge to stop Friend, whisper in his ear, 'I've got a pecker,' just to see if he would laugh and cool down, but somehow it didn't seem the time. Instead, he screwed his face into a thoughtful pose.

"You believe me?"

Friend looked at him, incredulous. "Of course I believe you, you nincompoop. Your whole story is full of DeBack's favorite ruses. You'd think he'd get tired of them, but no, time after time..."

"So, you've known him quite a while," Concho said in all innocence, hoping to focus in on the truth inside Friend with his thought beam. "Does that mean his dinosaur story is true?"

Friend stopped, pointed his finger in Concho's face. "Don't you mess with me, Boy. We ain't through dancin' here, not by a long shot."

'Well, what do you want from me? I already told you everything I know."

Friend shook his head. "You know one more thing."

"What's that?"

"Where is DeBack going?"

He looked Friend right in the eye. He suddenly had the seasick feeling of having one foot on either side of some cosmic teeter-totter.

DeBack/Friend.

Friend\DeBack.

DeBack/Friend.

His head began to ache. He covered his ears with his hands, closed his eyes and spoke in a whisper. "Are you a good guy or a bad guy?"

Friend moved closer, his face inches from Concho's. His breath was like eggs gone just a little off.

"Neither. I'm just here doing a job."

"For who?"

Friend smiled. "For whom? *Whom* do you think?"

Concho pondered, nodding his head like a junkie. "See, that's what I don't get." He motioned with his head upward. "If He's so all powerful, what the hell's this hubbub down here?"

Friend sighed, one of those long, drawn out, here-we-go-again sighs.

"It's a lot different than you think." He snorted. "And it keeps changing. Both good and evil have rules. And that dadblasted snake keeps dancing on either side, busting up the rules for both. There is order to the universe as long as we keep DeBack in check."

"What is he, Satan or something?"

Friend went white and appalled as though he'd been slapped. "No, he's not Satan."

Concho leaned forward in his chair, animated. "How do you know? Hell, as far as I can see, DeBack's the perfect choice, got all the attributes..."

"He isn't Satan."

"How do you know?"

"Because I..." Friend's nose touched the end of Concho's. The smell of just-off eggs was even more powerful, "...*he* ain't."

Concho stared, his own nose fighting against the putrid air between him and Friend. Had the man really just winked?

The right Reverend brushed his hands, picked up his pet, and snapped the locks on his briefcase. Looked over at Concho, a lawyer to his client. "If you're ready, Mr. Concho, I suggest we get going we have little time to waste in finding your friend, DeBack."

"Look, this is all kinda balled up inside me," Concho said, hoping to stall.

"Listen up. I've got a job and you've gotta job. You've gotten a little off track, that's all. That conjuring business back in Texas? He sucked you outta somewhere—or nowhere would be better—and brought you here. You're neither dead nor alive, you're in a kind of spiritual half-way house. Don't look so uptight, it's an old trick. And I can tell you he's got one or two more up his sleeve. But this time it's checkmate. And I'm...No, no, make that you. You're gonna pick up the check."

Concho's thought beam was picking up a disturbing image of DeBack. And yet it was no DeBack he recognized.

"Destiny awaits, Mr. Concho. Destiny sure as hell awaits."

♌♌♌

Phil Williams sat with a bottle of scotch, an ashtray full of cigarettes next to him, and his bleary eyes focused on the television monitor.

A fixed camera showed Oprah Rivera Springer and President Panic holding up their hands while the voice of the space station chaplain intoned the wedding vows.

"Do you, Oprah Rivera Springer take this man to be your lawful wedded husband, until death do you part?"

A tear ran down her/his cheek and caught in the underbrush of her/his mustache.

"I do."

"And do you, President Steven Rajpur Panic take this... this..."

"Person," interjected his betrothed.

"Uh... this person to be your lawful wedded... uh..."

"Spouse," came from the petulant talk show host/ess.

"Spouse."

"I did earlier and I do now." Panic grinned, as she/he swatted him playfully on the shoulder.

"I now pronounce you... man and... married."

Panic leaned over and kissed her/him. He moved away and grinned as he pulled a hair from between his teeth. A launch control announcer's voice intruded.

"Ten__Nine__Eight_"

Panic closed his eyes. Oprah slipped the aviator goggles over hers and waved to the camera.

"Seven_Six_Five_Four_"

"What a honeymoon!" Oprah Rivera Springer Panic shouted as the engines revved.

Williams reached for the bottle and took a long drink as the space station reverberated with the launch. A second camera attached outside the station showed the progress as the rocket—normally used for two-man exploration teams—headed toward the friction flare of the asteroid.

Williams' life-long ambition was about to come true.

The rocket reached the asteroid, glowed for a moment, then burst into a mighty fireball as it collided with the colossal rock.

Somewhere down the hall of the space station, a plaintive bugle sounded taps.

Williams gave a low, muttering laugh. "That, that person must not've been the second Adam after all."

He smiled evilly and took another swig from the bottle and stood, stretching. He was now alone and drunk and very much the president of the United States of America. At least for the next twenty-four hours. He might not go down in the history books, since there would soon be no history books, but damn it, he was the chief executive of the United States of America. He could do whatever he wanted.

He wobbled blearily to an intercom on the wall and pressed a button. He burped and said in a thick, fruited voice, "I wanna declare war on... s-somebody." He spied the nearly empty bottle sitting on the table. "Scotchland. I wanna declare war on... on them and..." He paused and his unfocused eyes wandered across the ceiling. "And I wanna make stuff legal...and I wanna..."

"Sir?"

Williams lurched, startled. He eyed the intercom suspiciously. He pressed the button again. "Whozat?"

"Sir, you wanted what?"

"I'll tell you what I want!" he bellowed, and lost his balance for a moment and fell backward against the table and slid to the floor.

"I'll tell you what I want...I want my...my wife back," he mumbled. He pursed his lips and wiped at a sudden moistening in his eyes. "I want Angel back. Please. Very much please. I miss her desperately."

In his misery, he glanced out the large porthole at the asteroid. A long dark finger of smoke was reaching out to him. Beckoning? He rose unsteadily, staggered to the window just as the smoking finger and debris reached the space station.

Sweat poured down his neck as the temperature rose in the cabin. He wheeled and started for the door. Halfway there he fell to his knees, forgetting where he was headed.

A moment later, his lungs seared and he vaguely remembered standing next to a volcano during his honeymoon.

"Angel," he whispered once. Then there was no more air.

♌♌♌

Angel Williams pushed herself away from the table at the Paradise Cafe, looked at Colonel Ross. Her clown-face was smeared with barbecue sauce. She licked her lips, threw her head back and laughed.

"You just gotta love this planet."

Ross took each of her hands, dipped the fingers into the bowl of warm water and wiped them carefully with a red towel. He then took the towel and wiped her face. She raised each hand upon completion, inspected them, then grinned.

"Good work, soldier."

"The pleasure is mine."

"First ribs, now eight ball." She motioned to the waiter. "Bring me another apple daiquiri in the pool room."

She grabbed her glass, swaggered across the restaurant, and pushed open the door into the green felt jungle.

"All right, boys, who's looking to get their butt beat?"

A general round of laughter met her challenge. One man alone in a far corner continued playing. She sauntered over, stood in his direct line-of-sight as he bent at the waist, squinting, beady eyed, measuring his next shot. *Clak*. He sank a three knock combination and left himself a straight-in.

"Not bad," she said. "You any good one-on-one?"

He raised up from the table, taking his time, his eyes meeting her. His smile was one of recognition, a shared joke.

"You might say I invented one-on-one, my dear."

Angel breathed deeply, as if struck by g-forces, feeling the air come from the farthermost part of her. Her toes and fingers curled, other parts opened. She felt faint.

"You...?"

He smiled, revealing perfect teeth. He was a darkly tanned, ruggedly handsome man dressed in a comfortably faded shirt, jeans and boots.

"That's right, Darlin'." He reached out his hand. "I'd love to shoot a game with you. Can't imagine the stakes." He winked. "But what's say we see what we can do about saving this planet from that rotten ol' asteroid?"

Still in shock, she took his hand, mesmerized by the face, the build. She might forget names, but Angel never forgot the feel of someone between her legs. Even if it had been ages ago.

He'd been there first. At the beginning of everything.

Colonel Ross stepped into the room. "Angel, are you okay?"

She nodded. "Yes. This is...is..."

The man stuck out his hand. "They've been calling me Concho, this time 'round. Glad to meet you." He studied Ross. "You a pilot or something?"

"Or something."

"Got access to a plane?"

"Yes."

"One that'll take us to Texas real fast?"

"For a good enough reason, yes."

Concho pointed to the sky. "How's that for a reason?"

Ross eyed him for a long moment, searching for signs of bluff or deceit.

"Can you stop it?"

"I think so."

"How?" Angel asked.

"You just get me to Texas, where a feller named DeBack has himself a cave. You get me there, I'll show you how."

Ross looked at Angel.

She nodded, her lips tight. Determined. "Air Force One?"

Ross shook his head, looking at his complex military watch. "We need something a whole lot faster. Come on."

Angel walked between the two men, hand-in-hand with both, glad she'd finally come back to earth.

"Lord a'mighty," the man who called himself Concho said, as they walked. "You just wouldn't believe the last couple days."

As they left, the television showed a picture of empty blue space, where once the government had circled in safety. Then the camera swiveled and the screen was filled with the image of the dark approaching rock.

♌♌♌

Clifford Clemp saw Zwetlot motioning to him from down what looked like a mile-long hallway. He rose, staggered through a small forest of long-stemmed glasses. "Powerful seltzer water here in New York," he murmured. He traversed the treacherous hallway by bouncing back and forth between the two walls. A large fern took a swing at him. A plush-covered chair leaped in his path.

Zwetlot looked concerned when he saw Clemp's face.

"What's the matter?"

"You're drunk," Zwetlot said, disgusted.

"'Cited, that's all. First big gig."

"Blotto. Smashed. Liquefied."

"Bringing in the sheaves, bringing in the sheaves," Clemp sang, "we shall come rejoicing, bringing in the sheaves."

"You know what you gonna tell them?"

Clemp nodded. Patted his jacket, it glimmered brightly.

"Got it right here, brother, safe and sound."

"You gonna read your sermon."

Clemp shook his head. "No paper. Heart," he belched gaseously. "Got it here in my heart."

"You know this is a once-in-a-lifetime opportunity."

"You're tellin' me," Clemp nodded, one eye twitched and he burped again. He staggered on stage into the bright lights and slowly raised his arms toward heaven.

"Is everybody happy?" he called out.

"Yes!" they shouted back.

"Do you wanna help me turn back that asteroid?"

"Hell, yes!"

He blinked twice, three times. Show time.

"Then let me hear you say, 'Jesus is my savior!'"

♌♌♌

The SR-171 set a new record taking the couple to Love Field in Dallas, where a waiting helicopter sped them to what Concho kept referring to as DeBack's cave.

"Here, here it is!" He called over the noise of the chopper. He pointed to a large triangular shaped knoll.

The pilot gave a stoic nod and slowly brought the helicopter down on top of the small hill overlooking the entrance to DeBack's cave. As the struts came in contact with the ground a fierce gust of wind shook them. The pilot took off his headset, setting the blades to the off position.

"I don't think you've got long," he shouted over the wind.

"Ah, it's always windy in West Texas," Angel's companion expressed smoothly, as if trying to ease her mind. "Comes at you like an eggbeater. From all directions."

"Here, take these flashlights," the colonel said, handing one to each of them. "Looks dark in the cave."

Angel hopped out close behind the man who called himself Concho. The asteroid loomed huge in the sky, its round nose not quite making contact with the earth's outer atmosphere, but glowing blood red.

"Not long now," he shouted to Angel, gripping her hand. "Maybe twenty minutes. That's all the time we got."

The air roared and the entire planet seemed to shake.

The man she recognized from so deep within herself led her down to the mouth of the cave. They shined their lights around in the dark cave's huge outer vestibule looking for the torch.

"Look," he said finally, pointing his flashlight toward the first glyph of Adam and Eve and the serpent. "Tell me if this looks familiar?"

Instinctively, like an infant reaching out in the darkness for light, she extended her hand toward it.

"Don't touch it," he whispered. "It has a kind of power. They all do," his arm sweeping across the thousands of glyphs.

Angel shook her head, fighting back tears, turning away. "We made a real mess of things, didn't we?"

He took her arms and gently turned her back around. "Yes we did, but remember, it was his fault," he hissed. "That snake. This time, it'll all be different."

For a moment she shook her head violently, her hair falling in her face, overwhelmed by the on-rush of eons-old memories, events that were buried deep within her and never meant to return to the surface.

"You think it'll ever be like that again?" she asked. "The Garden? Our beautiful garden?"

"We can make one. It won't be the same, but with any luck maybe it'll be better."

She breathed deeply, regaining her control, her sense of purpose.

"Okay. How's 'bout we stop that damn asteroid." she said fiercely. "And make a new start."

"I'm with you there, baby."

"So, what do we have to do?"

He walked to where a rock jutted at an angle from the cave wall. He reached his arm behind it, up to the shoulder and pulled the ancient mummified treasure from it's hiding place "All you have to do is eat this," he said.

"A yucky, shriveled up apple?" Angel screwed up her face and looked at him. "Are you sure?"

He nodded. "It's the only way."

As she struggled with a sense of wrongness, a lone figure stepped from behind a bend in the cave wall.

"No, Angel. It isn't the only way."

Startled, Angel looked at the stranger. Wait. This was no stranger, he looked familiar in a slick, face-lifted way. Television, maybe?

"Who're you?"

"Reverend Friend, at your service, Mrs. Williams." He inclined his upper torso a touch.

"Why don't you tell her your real name," her companion chimed in.

The Reverend stared hard. "You first."

"All right," he said with a flinty smile. "Concho's the name. Though I used to be called Adam." He put the pruny apple in Angel's hand. "Come on, baby, the clock's ticking."

Angel held the apple, never taking her eyes off Reverend Friend. Even from this distance she could smell the foul eggs scent. Sulfur.

"I know you! You're not just a TV preacher, you're really... *him*, aren't you? You, you prevaricator!"

"As a matter of fact," Friend nodded, "I am *him*"

She put the apple to her lips. "Give me one good reason why I shouldn't eat this apple."

Friend motioned with his head and another figure came from around the bend, carrying a good-size box.

The new figure was the spitting image of the man who stood beside her. Angel felt another urgent, aching tug at her insides.

"Hello, my love," he said, in the same voice as the Concho next to her. "I really don't think you want to eat that."

"Why not?" Angel asked, dazed. Glancing wildly from one man to the other and then down at the apple.

"Because, you're too beautiful to spend the rest of eternity as a snake."

The wind picked up outside. Black clouds of fine dust swirled through the opening of the cave. Angel looked at the Concho beside her, the look-alike holding a box near Reverend Friend—whom she now recognized for who he really was.

"Why should I believe you, when you're obviously working with him?" She motioned toward Friend.

"Good question. But the answer is simple." The look-alike nodded. "He has more to lose than any of us."

She shook her head. "I don't get it."

"Eat the apple," the man she'd entered the cave with said, gripping her hand with increasing pressure. "There's not much time."

"If the earth is destroyed," the person with the box said, "that snake pretending to be a man standing next to you has to face God with the rest of us. All of us—you, me, everyone who has ever lived, even Reverend Friend here—has faced our Maker at least once since the world was created. But that snake never has. He's got a heap of explainin' to do, and I don't imagine that would be very pleasant for him, do you?"

Angel looked to the Concho beside her. He frowned, shaking his head.

The man with the box stepped forward. "You and I are those who will become one. We'll save the world from the asteroid, together."

She stared hard at the man holding her hand, looked to the one with the box.

"He has no way of melding with you," that Concho said. "Only I can do that. Only I exist in that half-way place between life and afterlife." He smiled, then pointed at his twin. "Tell her how you conjured me."

"This is some kind of sick joke." The man beside her gripped her hand. "Only I can fulfill the prophecy, my Angel. Things'll be different this time around. Believe me."

"Enough talk!" roared Reverend Friend. "Proving time is here."

"You can't prove anything," Her Concho squeezed Angel's hand harder.

The man with the box stepped forward, knelt down and started opening it. "I think I can."

"How's that?"

He opened a crack, exposing a small animal, looked up and grinned. "There's only one thing in the world that a snake really hates."

"What?" Angel and the man with her said simultaneously.

"That, my dear Eve," the man opened the lid further and a small furry creature jumped out, snarling, "is a Mongoose."

Angel screamed when the Concho standing next to her roared and the mongoose sank its teeth into his pant leg. He shook his leg twice, then headed for the cave opening, his clothes seemingly melting off him as he ran. Even without sharing the apple in Angel's hand—the very last West Texas apple—he sloughed his human form and slithered in an eye blink out into the raging storm.

"Eve...er, Angel...I'm the only one who can save the world from that asteroid. Bring his bag and follow me, shine your flashlight along the cave floor," the real Concho shouted, running toward the back of the cave, torch in hand.

History swirled past him: Zulu wars and richly robed kings and woolly mammoths and Greek philosophers; French kings; a succession of Popes; a heavy-set Chairman Mao swimming in the Yangtze River; a vulture-eyebrowed Richard Nixon holding up his fingers, asking the cave walls to "trust me."

Concho concentrated on a single moment, a single place, as the past flurried around him. His brain seemed to swell inside his head again.

At last the swirling slowed and DeBack's recorded history flew off in different directions. Before him was the dividing line where the present and future met. There it was. A glyph of the asteroid, like a stone unhewn by human hands ready to smash into the Earth's rounded surface. Unsteadily, Concho leaned against the wall, holding the torch in one hand. Blood pounded in his skull. Salty sweat dropped into his eyes. He blinked back the stinging pain.

He reached out for the bag Angel was carrying.

Muscles taut, he leaned back and with his free hand, knocked the large bluish stone against the glyph with all his might, sending out a shower of sparks. Again he pulled back and smashed the rock against the etched asteroid.

The earth trembled so violently Concho nearly lost his balance. He smashed, and smashed the rock a second time, a third time, against every innocence lost, every money grubbing congressman, every religious war, every wasted life. Clouds of dust rolled off the serpent's wall. Tiny shards of stone buried themselves in his face, his eyes.

Finished at last, he grabbed Angel's hand and they stumbled toward the front of the cave.

"The storm hasn't let up," Angel shouted over the tumult. "Could you have missed something?"

He glanced back at the glyph. Totally obscured. He looked at Angel, shrugged.

"Maybe it's destiny."

"Couldn't be." She shook her head. "God wouldn't do things this way."

Then Concho spotted it on the floor of the cave's large vestibule. The mummified apple. He looked up at Friend, who remained standing in the corner.

"That asteroid's looking for me, ain't it?" Concho said.

Friend nodded.

"Adam...Concho...what?"

Concho leaned over and picked up the apple. "I eat this, I go back to where I came from, right?"

"More or less," Reverend Friend said.

"Damn." Concho shook his head.

"What are you talking about?" Angel took his arm. "Remember what happened the last time you took a bite of one of those..."

"I know, Darlin'," Concho smiled. "But last time, my being here was God's idea... Whatever DeBack did to conjure me up, he broke some kind of natural rule."

"Don't!" Angel cried. "What if it's another trick? A trap? What if *you* turn into a snake?"

Concho smiled. "Then many generations of feminists will have been right about me."

"That's not funny."

"I know, Darlin'." Concho grew serious, held the apple to his lips. "I just want you to know one thing."

"Yes?"

"I have loved you through all times past." He started to take the bite, then stopped. "And I will love you through all future times."

He bit and chewed, bit and chewed, filling his mouth with the meat of the dried apple. He closed his eyes, sank to his knees.

"No matter what happens." Angel lifted his chin to look at his face. "I love you too, Darlin'."

She held him in a tight embrace as the storm howled and screamed beyond the cave walls. The sound engulfed her and she closed her eyes. Her very atoms seemed to be shattering from the intensity of the noise. Then, just as the storm seemed to reach a pitch, all went silent.

She blinked twice. Looked down. Her arms were empty.

♌♌♌

"Say it again, brothers and sisters," Clifford Clemp raised his arms, framed against the largest window of the Rainbow Room. Outside, the sky was fire and light, a swirling extravaganza better than any Fourth-of-July fireworks show ever put on, even during the Koch era. "Jesus is my savior!"

The crowd roared. Clemp put his hand to his ear.

"I can't hear you!"

Another roar.

Clemp turned to the window, fell to his knees and reached toward the center of the firestorm, his palms upright.

"In the name of everything holy and good, I beg of you, Lord, let this messenger of death pass by our door."

The storm grew. The building shook as if it were a tree being uprooted by the wind. The crowd screamed in unison. People began moaning and crying, gnashing their teeth and tearing at their clothing.

Again Clemp threw up his hands.

"Be gone, I say to you. This day belongs to the Lord."

Norman Zwetlot tumbled at Clemp's feet, thrown from his seat by the shock waves the ten mile diameter rock made as it rocketed through space.

"Begone, and let us live another day!" cried Clemp, his eyes closed in fierce prayer. "I command you!"

In an instant, the storm ceased. The red storm swallowed itself in a single gulp and the tremors stopped.

Clemp opened his eyes, patted his body, looked out the window at a serene, late evening sky. Soon to be another balmy New York day.

"Holy rabbit poop," he whispered to himself. "It worked."

♌♌♌

Saleem closed his eyes and wafted dreamily with the aroma in the air. He had never seen so many roses. He nervously straightened his tie, leaned over and grinned at the reporter next to him as questions were fired one-after-another at the podium.

"This is my first day as a reporter in America," Saleem said. "It is exciting to participate in such an historical moment."

The reporter shrugged. "Whatever. Yeah, sure, Kid."

The President reached for a glass of water to the left of the microphones, glanced across the crowd with a beaming smile.

"After six months in space, there surely is nothing like fresh, *unfiltered* water."

There was a smattering of laughter, then a few seconds of quiet.

"Just one more question."

The reporter next to Saleem raised his voice above the eager crowd. "Will your startling election by unanimous vote via the internet signal a new era in American politics?"

Angel nodded and took a moment.

"Well, I truly appreciate the sentiments of the electorate." She paused, lowered her head for a moment. "But before people get too carried away thinking I did anything especially brave or noteworthy by coming back when I did, I want to go on record saying that what President Steven Panic and Oprah Rivera Springer did was far braver."

"Even though what they did knocked the space station and your husband out of the sky?" came from a surly woman's voice in the back of the crowd.

"Yes, well, the fact that it also led to the destruction of the space station doesn't diminish their act." She gazed upward for a moment, then shook herself as if from a reverie. "For we now know their mission succeeded. The asteroid must have taken longer than we anticipated to break apart and scatter after the nuclear explosion. All I can say is that we owe our fallen president and his...spouse our deepest thanks for sparing our planet from certain destruction."

"And just who do we thank for that chunk of space junk that clobbered Awareness, Missouri?" again the surly voice.

Angel craned her neck to finally spy the speaker, a huge, flush-faced woman who was whispering fiercely to a large English sheep dog next to her. The president tried to hide a grin as the woman fought to disengage the dog's front paws from around her massive thigh.

"I've made a note," Angel said, coughing with laughter, "to check on relief efforts as soon as this press conference is concluded.

"Enough, Bobby," the woman commanded through clenched teeth.

"Yes, well." Angel cleared her throat, gazed her most statesman-like gaze. "If there are no more questions."

When it was clear that she had finished, the mob of reporters began leaping up and down like jack rabbits looking for one last piece of lettuce in a bare patch.

"That's all for now, gentlemen, ladies," she said with a wave and started back inside.

"Madam President! Madam President!"

President Angel Williams gazed across the mass of sweating, note-pad clutching reporters. Her eyebrows lifted. She smiled and nodded toward the speaker as she spoke.

"My daughter told me to be sure that I allowed a very special reporter to ask a question at my first official press conference," she said, pointing to a youngish-looking, Arabic version of Sam Donaldson.

"Yes, Saleem...uh...Sam?"

Saleem stood slightly forward, suddenly the picture of dignity, straight as a two-by-four.

"Will you be holding all your future press conferences here in the Rose Garden?" The question rushed out before he could consciously form the words in his mind.

There was a collective groan from the grizzled professionals. "Leave it to an amateur to blow the opportunity of a lifetime," one reporter grumbled.

Angel's attention shifted to the grumbling reporters, "And what were you going to ask me? Questions of great importance. Like what about social security? Will we ever pay off the national debt? And who's going to be the First Husband? What's the..."

The President's smile warmed, a knowing glint in her eyes as they locked onto Sam. Turning, she waved her arms. "The roses are beautiful aren't they Sam."

She moved closer to him. "Don't worry it was a good question. But you know Sam, there's one observation I've made recently, and that is you must never trust a garden snake, or any snake leaving footprints."

She turned again toward the White House doors where Colonel Ross held out an apple daiquiri to her.

"The Car is waiting to take us to Paradise for barbecued ribs," he whispered.

A long-time member of the Abilene Writers Guild, Vivian has plenty of experience chasing snakes as a girl growing up in Oklahoma, as a rancher raising three sons in Oregon and later as a realtor in Southwest Texas. This is her first novel.

9 781892 323026